THE DREAM HOME

THEO BAXTER

INKUBATOR
BOOKS

Published by Inkubator Books
www.inkubatorbooks.com

Copyright © 2024 by Theo Baxter

Theo Baxter has asserted his right to be identified as the author of this work.

ISBN (eBook): 978-1-83756-431-6
ISBN (Paperback): 978-1-83756-432-3
ISBN (Hardback): 978-1-83756-433-0

THE DREAM HOME is a work of fiction. People, places, events, and situations are the product of the author's imagination. Any resemblance to actual persons, living or dead is entirely coincidental.

No part of this book may be reproduced, stored in any retrieval system, or transmitted by any means without the prior written permission of the publisher.

PROLOGUE

"It's gone," I murmur shakily. "It's really gone."

My mind is a mess. I'm pretty sure it's broken and unrepairable. It doesn't matter. A small part of it remains somewhat sane and that's all I need. I don't know how long I've been here; it feels like years. I need to get out of here. I'm going to die if I don't. It'll kill me. I know it will.

My wrists are chained, but I figure I can break free with a piece of the wire from the cot the monster lets me sleep on sometimes. With the monster gone, I don't have to worry about it stopping me. I pull the mattress off the bed and attack the wires that held the mattress. I don't have anything to cut them with, so I just start yanking, twisting and turning. They aren't very thick. It takes me forever to finally get one end free.

My fingers are bloody as I stick the end in the keyhole of the lock on my wrist and start wiggling it, trying to trigger the lock. Finally, the cuff on my wrist opens. Elation fills me. I get to work on my other wrist, and it doesn't take near as long. Then I work on my ankles.

My heart is pounding as I race for the door and enter a long hallway. There are doors on either side of me and I test each one, but they each lead to another room, not out of this place.

I get to the end of the hall and try the last door. It opens on a staircase. I go up and push the door at the top. It shifts and I'm in some kind of family room. I see another set of stairs and I race up them too, shoving open the door. I'm in a house. A house with windows that look out on a big yard and the sun is streaming in through them. I haven't seen the sun in forever.

My eyes blur. I am nearly free. I turn and see the kitchen and I'm suddenly starved. I ransack the kitchen and eat everything I can to satiate my hunger. I have time. The monster said it would be gone for a while. That was yesterday. At least I think it was yesterday. Hours pass differently down below.

After filling my belly, I go to the door in the kitchen, but it won't open. Locked? I think. I try to figure out how to unlock it, but there isn't a manual unlock to the door. It needs a key.

Shaking, I hurry to the other doors in the house, but they are all the same. Every one of them has to be opened with a key.

"No!" I scream as I bang on the door. I'm still trapped in this nightmare. I pick up a chair and try to throw it out of the window in the front, but it just bounces off and smashes into the lamp on the table and falls to the floor.

This can't be happening. I can't be trapped here. I have to get away!

It dawns on me I had seen a phone in the kitchen, a landline... I run to it and pick it up... But it's dead, no dial tone. I yank it from the wall and throw it at the window in the kitchen, but it just does the same thing the chair did and lands on the floor.

Anger and rage consume me, and I destroy everything in my path the way that thing destroyed me.

And when it returns, I'll kill the grotesque creature and make my escape.

All I have to do now is wait.

usual since he traveled all over California because of his business—all excited, carrying a bunch of papers.

"What is it?" she asked, curious about his behavior.

As it turned out, he'd stumbled upon a great piece of land nestled in the forest. It was secluded, with nothing else around for miles.

"I thought we would stay on the lake," she said.

"I don't want our kids so close to the water. They could drown," he said matter-of-factly.

It was a good point. A lot of people drowned every year. Mostly drunken idiots, but accidents still happened.

"But this is the right place for us," he continued, pure passion sparkling in his eyes.

Ashlyn had nodded, excited by the prospect of building their own home.

Mason managed to buy the land in no time. There was an old house on the property that Mason tore down immediately so he could build their new home from scratch.

Ashlyn had never seen him like that before. So passionate and determined. He loved his job, but this was something else entirely. He was on a mission, a personal quest, and she found it endearing.

Mason was a well-known architect, and with that kind of prestige came wealth. He had a bunch of awards that he kept in his office. He said that stroked the ego of his future clients, and he could make more money, and she could see the logic behind his words.

His was one of the leading firms in the country, and he worked hard to maintain such levels of excellence. But he still made time for her and for creating the perfect home for her. He was devoted to that idea. Although Ashlyn didn't believe something like that was possible, she fell in love with her husband even more while watching him create a home for them; a place for their family.

Mason designed everything—the look of the house, each room just the way she would like it, including a working space for her in the attic. She had practically the whole floor all to herself for her brand-new business.

After graduating from Sierra Nevada University, she'd had no clue what she wanted to do with her life. Mason had suggested interior design. She liked the idea, and it started from there. She was over the moon when Mason asked that their home be her first big project, because she could later use it as a showcase of her skills.

Ashlyn put her heart and soul into creating the perfect home for them. It helped that Mason told her to spare no expense when choosing furniture, art pieces, and everything else a modern household required.

The only downside to this dream house project was that Mason was an extreme perfectionist. He demanded that everyone do everything the way he wanted it, without compromise.

Ashlyn had never been around a home being built, so she was taken aback when Mason had told her there were foundation problems. She hadn't understood why things were delayed and she was anxious to see the house making progress. But that wasn't the only issue early on. Soon after the framing went up, Mason had explained the contractors were having difficulties getting the water and sewer lines in. She could tell that he was extremely frustrated about it all and she had to admit she was as well, since she was anxious to have the house completed.

Because of the issues, Mason spent a lot of time on-site, making sure everyone did their jobs the right way. Ashlyn had wanted to be out there with him, but he'd said a building site was no place for a lady and that he wanted her to be surprised at the final outcome, which she'd found sweet, so she'd stayed away.

Instead, she'd focused on the specs he'd given her and ordered all the furniture, paint, and flooring. She used a computer program to design the rooms and show him how she wanted things arranged. She knew she could move things around once she was there. He'd approved everything she'd ordered, from the carpets and wall paint for each room to every last little knickknack, saying he trusted her judgment and that it would all look as beautiful as she was.

Just thinking about their new home had her excited to see it all in person, and today was the day that was going to happen.

THE DRIVE WAS ABOUT AN HOUR. She hadn't noticed how far from the city they would be when Mason had driven her out to the new property when he'd first bought it for them. She had been too excited at the thought of building their forever home. Now she was just a little bit worried about being so far from everything. Glancing at Mason, she shook her head. There was no reason for her to be upset. She had Mason to protect her, and it would be nice to be surrounded by Mother Nature.

Mason hummed to himself as he drove, and that made her smile.

"What?" he asked after a sidelong glance.

"It's good seeing you like this," she replied.

"Like what?"

"Happy."

He took her hand, kissing her knuckles. "Of course I'm happy. I finally get to show you the house and we get to start our family in the proper way," he declared.

"You're so sweet." His words made her giddy with excitement.

Mason made a turn off the main road. The trees were closer to them now. After a while going upward, he slowed down. "We're here," he announced, releasing her hand.

Ashlyn looked at the gray fence in front of her. "You didn't tell me you added such a high fence to the property," she noted as massive metal gates started to open. Of course, Mason had made them accessible by remote control so they wouldn't have to leave their vehicles during the cold season. *He's truly thought of everything.*

"It made sense. A lot of wild animals roam around here, and I want to make sure you're safe," he replied with a shrug.

She agreed in theory, but in practice, she hoped such a structure wouldn't hinder their view of the scenery, but as they drove through the gates, she realized it wouldn't. The property was massive, and she'd be able to enjoy the views.

All thoughts about the scenery left her then because finally, in front of her, stood their house. *THE HOUSE.* And it took her breath away. The car barely stopped before she got out for a closer look. It was magnificent. Regal. Palatial. And it was hers.

The house was three stories high with a distinguished attic space and huge windows that overlooked the grounds. Although it was very modern in design, there were certain elements that breathed old-fashioned to her, which made sense, considering who had designed it. Mason was a modern man with a lot of traditional values. They were very compatible in that regard.

Ashlyn continued to soak it all in as Mason walked over and stood beside her. The ivory of the house itself, with dark wood framing, went perfectly with all the shades of green and brown around them. Mason had even made sure the landscaping around the house was perfect with splashes of colorful wildflowers.

She could picture herself growing old here with Mason while watching their kids grow up. She got so emotional that her eyes watered, and she dried them with the back of her hand.

"Don't cry, honey," Mason said, giving her a hug. "If there's something you don't like, we can change it."

"No, no, it's perfect. I can't help the tears. This is amazing," she replied honestly. "I love everything."

Mason laughed. "You haven't seen everything yet."

She looked him straight in the eyes. "I don't have to. I already know the rest is perfect as well. Because you made it."

He tucked her close and leaned down to kiss her. "Welcome home, sweetheart."

They made a full circle around the house so she could see everything that Mason had done. Ashlyn could hear birds chirping all around her and insects buzzing. The forest was alive. Everywhere around them, life was happening, and she adored it. All of it put a big smile on her face. Looking at the yard now, she was glad Mason had thought to put up the fencing, and it wasn't even that close to the house so she could still enjoy the yard.

"Mason, this is just perfect," she said, getting emotional all over again as they ended up on the back patio with the covered gazebo. She could see the fairy lights that were hung, and she couldn't wait to sit out here in the evenings and enjoy the firepit and comfy furniture.

"Is it everything you dreamed about?"

"It's better."

He smiled, taking her hand. "Come on, let's go back around to the front and I'll show you the inside."

She happily followed his lead.

Mason ceremoniously opened the door for her but wouldn't allow her to step inside.

She looked at him questioningly.

Without saying anything, he swept her into his arms and carried her over the threshold. "I want to do this right."

She laughed wholeheartedly before awarding him with a kiss. Her husband was such a silly man at times, which not a lot of people were privy to see.

Once he set her down and Ashlyn looked around, a gasp escaped her lips. The place looked even better than she'd pictured it. She walked through the living room. The furniture she'd chosen looked as though it was specifically made for the room. It was gorgeous, even if she said so herself.

"I told you this coffee table would fit perfectly next to the couch," she said proudly, because Mason had thought the place would look overcrowded.

However, she'd measured everything more than a hundred times, making sure there would be no mistakes. Especially since Mason wouldn't bring her here and she had to rely on imagination and sketches and her online program, which made her nervous. All the same, the result was even better than her wildest dreams.

"That is one of the reasons I love you," Mason countered.

"Because of my ability to choose the perfect furniture?" she deadpanned.

He chuckled before replying, "You're as meticulous in making this the most perfect home as I am."

"Oh, no. There's only one control freak in this relationship," she continued to tease.

Mason wrapped his arms around her waist, pulling her closer to him. "Seriously. I'm very proud of you."

Hearing that warmed her heart. "I'm proud of *us*," Ashlyn said in return.

They shared a long kiss, the first of many, she hoped, in their new home.

"Do you want to see the rest of the house?" he asked as they parted, and there was genuine excitement in his voice.

"Of course."

Each time they entered a different room, Ashlyn would declare it was her new favorite room, which Mason found highly entertaining.

It was especially hard to leave their new bedroom, but once they returned downstairs, she tried the last door in the hallway, and it was locked. That made her frown.

"That's my man cave," Mason explained, wiggling his eyebrows.

"It's locked," Ashlyn stated the obvious.

"I didn't want the deliverymen to get tempted and steal some of my toys," he said, getting serious.

Ashlyn rolled her eyes. "Boys and their toys," she said under her breath.

Mason chuckled. "Here, I'll show you." He unlocked the door and led her down. "See? Nothing special yet."

The room barely had anything in it. Just a comfortable looking couch and an entertainment center with a TV and some gaming equipment.

"Are you sure you don't want me to decorate it?" she asked.

He shook his head. "I'm good. I've got plans for it and I want it to be my space. Okay?"

Ashlyn smiled. It was as though he was asking permission. "Of course that's okay."

He kissed her and they returned to the hallway. "Do you want to see the sound system I installed? It will go nicely with the PS5. And I built a small wine cellar. I couldn't help myself."

Ashlyn pretended to fall asleep. "I'll pass."

He kissed her again and laughed. "Do you want to settle into your office?"

She grinned. "You read my mind."

Mason nodded, kissing her brow. "Go then, and while you unpack, I'll make some business calls. Later, I'll order us dinner."

"So bossy."

"You know you love it."

"I absolutely do," Ashlyn replied, kissing her husband one more time out of sheer happiness.

Afterward, they went their separate ways. She went upstairs while Mason remained on the ground floor where his office was.

A few hours later, Mason surprised her with a romantic meal in their new dining room, after which they went upstairs and made love in their new bed. She was blessed to have such a perfect husband.

Ashlyn happily fell asleep nestled in Mason's arms but woke in the middle of the night to see him get out of bed and get dressed. He walked out of the room, and she turned to the other side, trying to return to sleep.

Mason suffered from insomnia, and he didn't like disturbing her, so he usually left the room. She knew he'd probably go watch TV or maybe he'd go down to his new man cave and play one of his video games. The thought made her smile.

She heard the door off the kitchen open. *Maybe he wanted to go for a walk,* she thought. They could do that now in the privacy of their property, and that put another smile on her face before she fell asleep again.

2

Ashlyn had always worried about Mason and his insomnia. She'd noticed over the years that it was worse the more stressed he was, and she was at a loss as to how to help. She hoped being in their new home would help him.

He worked a great deal and had a stressful job in which everything depended on him because he was the founder of the firm and the lead architect, so on one hand, it was no wonder he had trouble sleeping. On the other, he refused to see a doctor or get sleeping pills. Ashlyn wasn't sure if that was a man thing or a Mason thing. *Probably both.*

Ashlyn hoped that their new home would put him at ease at least in some small way, and that he'd lose some of the tension since their dream house was finally completed, which meant one less thing to be stressed about, but after a week, she realized that nothing had changed.

Maybe he needs a little more time to relax and slow down, she mused.

All the same, they managed to settle into their new lives

and routines pretty quickly. Mason had to go to work earlier, but he made sure he was always home for dinner. And if he had some unfinished business, he did it over the phone or online in his new home office.

Ashlyn loved her new office as well. It was spacious and bright, and she truly felt creative and full of vigor by being there.

She did her best to set up her interior design business, called Ashlyn Designs, eager to start designing homes for her clients.

If I ever get a client.

The bottom line was that she wanted Mason to be proud of her. Although she lacked nothing in her life thanks to her husband, she wanted him to see that she was more than capable of making her own money.

They had had that talk at the beginning of their relationship, while she was still in college, about how he never expected her to work or not to work once they were married. She could do what she wanted; whatever made her happy. And she realized designing made her happy. The fact that she could potentially earn a lot of money with the right clientele was a major bonus.

Money had always been an issue in her family, or the lack of it, and she felt blessed that Mason provided her with such an environment where she didn't have to worry about it anymore. Though it did make her feel guilty at times.

Thinking of her family made her realize she already missed them. She missed her friends, too. Because of the move, and all the work around it, she hadn't had a chance to see any of them in a while.

Although she was happy to finally be here in her new home, she couldn't ignore how far away from her friends and family she was now. Seeing them would require some juggling, some fine maneuvering around her responsibilities. But she knew she would make it work.

And one of the brightest sides of having her dream home was that she could fully concentrate on her work without being involved in other people's drama. Perhaps it appeared selfish, but when they lived in the duplex, her mom called her each time her younger sister, Karina, acted out, and Ashlyn would rush home to play mediator. Or if one of her friends had relationship troubles, Ashlyn was the one they called to bring ice cream and a shoulder to cry on.

Of course, she liked having people who were dependent on her, but it was time to focus on herself for a change. That didn't mean she planned to neglect her family and friends. More to the point, she was slightly worried about how she would balance everything in her new life.

When she complained to Mason about how it would be more difficult to schedule outings with friends since not all of them were in South Lake Tahoe—some had moved to Tahoe City, even Reno, and the commute would be stressful —he shrugged it off.

"It's not that far, sweetheart, but if it's too much of a drive for you, just don't go." He smiled. "Besides, I like knowing you're here and I can come home and have you to myself."

At times, he had a strange sense of humor. She knew that was a joke considering he was never home. And that was no exaggeration. From the start of their relationship, he'd been frank with her about his job and what it meant to him. If she wanted to be with him, she had to come to terms with his long work hours. What made it easier for her to accept that was the fact that when he was with her, he was with her 100 percent. Still, she felt lonely when he was at work.

Nowadays, that only motivated her more to build her own career. It was important that she have her own life because sitting at home, alone in this huge house, waiting for him to return, held no appeal to her. And so, she poured everything she had into her business.

She was overjoyed when she booked her first client. Mrs. Donovan called after seeing Ashlyn's ad on social media. Ashlyn sent photos of her home so the woman knew what she could expect, and she was blown away.

Mrs. Donovan asked if Ashlyn could remodel her sitting room. After speaking with her for a while, going to visit her and seeing the space, Ashlyn asked her about her likes, dislikes, hopes, and wishes for the room. She started to get all kinds of ideas about the space, and that excited her.

"Mostly, I want to shake up things a little, add a splash of color." Mrs. Donovan was adamant.

Ashlyn immediately started working, driving around town finding all the perfect pieces to make Mrs. Donovan's sitting room perfect.

As she'd entered the paint shop to pick up the new wall color, she noticed a man a few doors down staring at her. The intensity of his gaze had her feeling creeped out, so she'd hung out in the shop for a while in hopes that the man would be gone when she returned to her car.

Over the next few days, she had the feeling that she was being watched and it made her so anxious she hurried through her tasks, wanting to get back home to the sanctuary of her perfect house with its secure fencing and huge metal gate.

Despite her anxiety over the weird feeling of being watched and followed while she was in town, which she couldn't prove was happening even though she'd kept herself on high alert, she managed to get everything ordered for Mrs. Donovan.

Throughout the week, Ashlyn had ordered the new furniture, hired a few handymen, painted the room, and replaced the carpeting with hardwood and a beautiful accent rug. After two weeks of working hard, her first client had a brand-new sitting room. The result was spectacular, and Mrs. Donovan was more than happy, giving her a little extra for her services.

Receiving her first check for a job well done made her jump with joy. She was grinning from ear to ear when she showed it to Mason. "I know it's nothing compared to what you earn for—"

"Are you kidding me? This is cause for celebration," he interrupted. "And I think you should definitely frame that. It's good luck."

"I think I just might do that."

The next day, after finishing with her workload, which wasn't that big since she was still looking for client number two, Ashlyn decided to call her family.

Skyping wasn't something she was used to doing when she lived within walking distance, but that was a small sacrifice considering all the gain.

Dialing up, she waited. The screen was completely dark, although she could definitely hear voices.

"You have to move out of the way, Mom," her sister protested.

"I know. I wasn't born in the previous century," her mother grumbled.

"Actually, you were," Karina and Ashlyn said at the same time, which made her smile.

"Oh, you know what I mean," her mom said, finally

moving away and sitting on the couch next to Ashlyn's father, readjusting the camera so she could see them perfectly.

"Hi, guys," Ashlyn said with a smile.

Was it just her imagination, or had her father gained a little weight? All the sitting around was definitely taking its toll.

Ashlyn's father, Brandon Dawson, had been a truck driver all his life, but he'd nearly lost his leg in a terrible accident last year. He still worked for the same company, but now he was an online salesman for trucking supplies.

Her dad was tough and resilient. He was the one who'd taught Ashlyn to never give up. He had some less-desirable traits as well, but she didn't hold that against him. He was her dad, and she loved him dearly.

"Can you hear us, Ashlyn? Can you see us?" her mom asked.

"Everything is great, Mom," she reassured with a thumbs-up.

Although her father had worked online for a while now, his PC was a dreadful old thing, and Ashlyn worried it could break down any minute. Sadly, her father was too proud to accept a gift from her such as a new computer. She knew they struggled with money to be able to buy a new one. So, Ashlyn pretended all was well.

Family dynamics were hard to navigate at times.

It didn't help that her father was the only one working. He was old-school like that. He believed a man should provide while a woman took care of the house, kids, and family.

Her mother, Melissa, was happy in that role as well. Her

only interests apart from her home were church and her precious TV shows.

Ashlyn teased her that she belonged to a completely different era. Her mom would huff in return.

Her mom squinted. "Are you all right? You look a little bit pale."

Ashlyn knew she could blame their old computer for the state of her appearance but decided not to go down that road. She didn't want to cause unnecessary tension. Finally, all was well in her parental home, and she wanted it to stay like that. "Settling into the new house wasn't easy. It took a lot of work. But I can't complain."

"You should have called us to help," her mom chastised.

"I didn't want to bother you."

"It's no bother. We're your family."

"I'm very happy here," Ashlyn said.

Her mom smiled. "That's good to hear."

"I'm thinking of putting in a garden," she shared, knowing how much her mom liked gardening.

Her mom nodded approvingly. "Are you eating enough?"

She had no idea from where her mom's ancestors came, but she was certain they were in some kind of a cult that was obsessed with food. "Of course I'm eating, Mom."

"Don't get all huffy. I need to ask. You look a bit skinny."

She always looked skinny to her mother. But Mason liked how she looked, so she took care of herself and made sure to maintain the same weight.

"And it's not like you have a market there in the middle of nowhere," she continued to grumble, snapping her from her thoughts.

"I'm just an hour away from you," Ashlyn pointed out.

"You're still too far away. What if something happens?"

This was the same talk they'd had for the past couple of years. Ashlyn knew that her mother took her moving away the hardest.

"The delivery of fresh groceries, including fruits and vegetables, comes to the house every week." Mason made sure of that. "And a lot of restaurants are willing to deliver as well." *As long as Mason tips them well.*

"Must be nice to be rich," Karina commented in the background.

Ashlyn couldn't see her younger sister, but she was definitely in the room. And so was her disapproval. She'd never liked Mason, and although it sounded awful, Ashlyn believed she was jealous. So far, all her relationships had been trainwrecks. Karina took the term *fall for a bad guy* to a whole new level.

Ashlyn had made a conscious decision to stop apologizing to her family for having a rich husband. Most parents would be glad their daughter had managed to escape that cycle of poverty, yet hers continued to regard wealth as something evil and Mason as someone who was untrustworthy because of it, which hurt her deeply.

She hoped that over time, their feelings would change when they saw how happy, taken care of, and cherished she was. So far, that particular miracle hadn't happened.

She asked her father how he was doing. As always, he was very frugal with his responses, keeping them short. She had no idea how he'd managed to sell anything since the man clearly didn't like speaking.

"Would you like a tour?" she asked next.

As expected, her mother nodded enthusiastically.

Picking up her laptop and carrying it throughout the entire house and then out the back door to show off the backyard, Ashlyn showed her family everything. She explained what precisely was done and why, and how she'd contributed.

The only place she skipped was Mason's man cave. Nobody in her family would be impressed with his video game collection. If anything, her father would dislike him even more knowing how he'd "wasted time on such foolish things." That was a direct quote from her father when she was in her preteens and asked for a game for Christmas.

She ended the tour by returning to her office on the top floor. "And this whole floor is all mine, where I work," she said proudly.

"I still don't understand why you need to work."

"That's because you're stuck in the 1950s," Karina deadpanned.

Her father ignored that, continuing to speak to Ashlyn. "Doesn't that husband of yours make enough money? Has he lied about being successful?" he grumbled.

Ashlyn had to work hard to rein in her temper. On one side, she knew her father meant well and was concerned about her well-being. On the other, it was infuriating that he constantly looked for reasons to dislike Mason.

"Everything is fine," she stressed. "And I don't *have* to work, Dad. I *want* to," she insisted.

Sadly, it was like talking to a wall. He did not get it, being so old-fashioned. His scoffing confirmed as much.

"You need to focus on other things and let your husband worry about money," he insisted.

Explaining to her father how life didn't have to be so rigid was a waste of time, so Ashlyn stayed quiet.

Karina decided to speak for her. "These are different times, Dad. Women can have it all, just like men do. Besides, if you let Mom work, perhaps we could afford a computer you didn't have to duct tape."

What?

"Or a new TV."

Her father frowned. "There's nothing wrong with my computer or my TV. They work just fine. That's all that matters."

"Yeah, which is a miracle considering they are the first things made in color," Karina said.

"Perhaps I could afford a new TV if you hadn't moved back home," he grumbled.

But Ashlyn knew he didn't mean that. When they were much younger, their father was pretty stern, but he was mellowing in his old age. Ashlyn knew how happy he was that Karina was home, and that she was trying to put her life back on track. Her rebellious years had brought them a lot of heartbreak, and it was good those days were finally behind them.

Come to think of it, since Karina was such a wild child, always testing the boundaries her father set for them, it was no wonder that Ashlyn turned out the way she had. She always tried to be perfect and not cause any problems because her sister already caused enough grievance to their parents for the both of them. She didn't want to be an extra burden. In the past, she'd resented Karina for that. She was allowed freedom Ashlyn never was, yet with time, she outgrew that way of thinking.

"I eat your food, too," Karina teased.

Her father shook his head. "Oh, you brat." Yet he was smiling.

Despite still having a smart mouth, her baby sister was

growing up, and Ashlyn was truly proud of her for enrolling in junior college.

"I can chip in for a new TV," Ashlyn offered, hoping that this time around, they would accept her help.

"That's okay, honey. We can manage," her mom was quick to reassure her. "Now tell me, how are the neighbors?"

The change of subject wasn't very subtle, but Ashlyn still went with it. "I don't have neighbors."

Her mother shook her head. "I don't like the thought of you all alone in the middle of nowhere. Mason is gone all day long, and that makes you vulnerable."

Mom's TV shows about bandits around every corner and scoundrels waiting to exploit young women made her fearful. If it weren't for that feeling she'd had of being followed and watched while she was in town, Ashlyn might have been inclined to scoff at her. She knew there were predators out there in the world, but of all the places she felt vulnerable, this house wasn't one of them.

"Between the security system Mason installed, unbreakable windows, and a freakishly large fence no animal can climb, I'm good. This place is as secure as a bank vault," she insisted. "I feel really safe here, Mom."

"If you say so," her mom replied with a sigh.

In other words, they would definitely revisit this topic in the future.

They spoke for a little longer before her mother had to make dinner, which made Ashlyn think she could do the same and surprise Mason with a home-cooked meal.

"Talk to you soon." She sent a bunch of kisses before closing her laptop and heading to the kitchen.

She was about done with dinner when she heard Mason's car approaching, and that put a smile on her face.

Perfect timing.

3

Mason came home from work a little earlier than usual, declaring that they should go out and finally celebrate the move-in.

"Haven't we already done that, like in every room of the house—actually, a couple of times in some of them?" Ashlyn joked.

He kissed the tip of her nose. "Funny. Still, I won't be derailed. I want to treat my wife, so go and get dressed."

"You should have called. I already made dinner."

He smiled. "And it smells delicious. Will it keep for tomorrow?" he asked.

She grinned as she pulled containers from the cabinet and started putting everything into them. "Sure. Let me put it away. You know, we could have met in the city, then you wouldn't have had to come all the way home."

"I know. But I like driving around with you."

"Weirdo." She giggled and put the last of the food away, then turned to him. "Move."

With a big smile on her face, she went up to their bedroom. However, entering her closet, she felt at a loss.

What the hell am I going to wear? Not knowing where they were going, it was a hard decision. And it didn't help that she had a lot to choose from. This whole closet was far bigger than her former bedroom in her parents' house. It was insane.

Mason spoiled her rotten, always buying her things. But she liked that about him, that he wasn't afraid to pick clothes for her. When he looked at her, she felt seen. He saw the real her, good and bad, and that was exciting.

"Wear that emerald-green dress I bought you last year," Mason yelled from the bedroom.

And it was helpful when he came to the rescue, saving her from a potential headache by choosing what she should wear.

Ashlyn nodded, although he couldn't see her. His choice was no surprise. He always liked to see her in green since it went nicely with her red hair, green eyes, and freckled face.

"Okay," she called. "Thank you," she added, slipping into the dress.

It clung to her body like a glove and was on the long side, with sleeves that were slightly off her shoulders. She wasn't showing a lot of cleavage, but it was definitely noticeable.

Ashlyn was relieved it still fit her perfectly because that meant she hadn't gained any weight. Come to think of it, she hadn't gained any weight since getting married, which she felt was a huge accomplishment because she'd struggled in the past. She was tall enough that she could definitely handle a few extra pounds, but Mason helped her stay in shape. He made sure her diet was full of healthy options and had a full gym inside the house so she could exercise any time she wanted to.

She hadn't had that growing up. She was obliged to eat whatever was provided because the alternative was going to bed hungry. That was not a critique of her parents, because she knew how they struggled, but usually those cheaper options weren't so healthy. Knowing that her parents still ate the same things worried her. Especially since her father struggled with high blood pressure and high cholesterol.

I will cook them a big dinner with a lot of fresh vegetables and the best quality meat, she promised herself.

Ashlyn did that every so often. She couldn't do it too frequently because they would know she was doing it for their benefit. However, if she said she was feeling lonely and wanted to spend time with them and cook for them, then everything would go smoothly. It was annoying that she had to trick them like that, as though they were her children, yet at the same time, she would do a lot more to take care of her family.

After zipping the dress all the way up, she chose some matching emerald earrings and was ready to go.

She left her closet carrying a pair of heels. She'd never particularly cared for those torture devices, but Mason liked them, and she had to admit they complemented her look like flats never could, so she endured.

Mason looked at her approvingly as she did a little twirl for him. "Stunning," he said.

Ashlyn's cheeks turned slightly pink. No matter how many times he complimented her, she always reacted in the same manner. He'd had that effect on her from the moment they met, which had been completely accidental.

He had visited her college, conducting some business, of

course. They wanted him to design the new science building, and as he walked on campus, she was there. It was a nice sunny day, so she'd been studying outside, lounging on a blanket under a tree. She always needed to stay in the shade with a lot of sunblock because her pale skin burned quite easily.

Mason had approached her. Without wasting any time on small talk or even asking for her name, Mason told her they would be going on a date.

Ashlyn was so stunned by this beautiful man dressed in a power suit that she nodded. He flashed one of his sexy smiles—it was just a tad arrogant, as though he knew she would react like that—and handed her his phone to put her number into it.

Ashlyn wasn't exaggerating when she said that remembering her phone number while those gray eyes looked at her with such intensity was the hardest thing in her life. However, after telling herself to calm down, the digits came to her. And then she established full-on eye contact as she returned the phone.

"You forgot to put your name in here," he noted.

Ashlyn cursed to herself. So much for playing it cool. She was acting like a complete idiot in front of this man. "It's Ashlyn," she said, finally finding her voice.

"Ashlyn the goddess," he mumbled as he typed.

She forgot how to breathe. *What did he say? Goddess?*

And then, he'd disappeared, promising he would call.

She just lay there, on the grass, with a pounding heart and her cheeks ablaze.

In a matter of days, they were dating, in a few months engaged, and married shortly after because Mason didn't want a long engagement. Ashlyn preferred it like that too since she couldn't wait to become his wife. They got married on the beach in Hawaii, and Mason was kind enough to fly her parents and her sister there as well so they could witness the ceremony. That helped with her parents accepting that she was marrying so soon, and to a man who was twelve years older.

Fast-forward five years, and nothing had changed. She was still madly in love with the man. Meeting Mason that day had been the best thing that happened in her entire life, and each day with him was a blessing.

"What are you thinking about that is putting such a big smile on your face?" Mason asked, snapping her from her thoughts.

"I was thinking about you. About the day we met."

"I knew you would be my wife then and there," he said matter-of-factly. "But I knew I would have to play it cool until you were madly in love with me."

"After five years, I finally hear about this master plan of yours," she teased.

"You don't know the half of it," he replied, winking.

"Thank you for the assistance, by the way. I struggled with what to wear."

"That is what I live for." He kissed her lips, then lingered there.

Having him so close sent shivers down her spine.

"Let's go. I want to be able to enjoy the sunset while we eat."

When Mason drove to their favorite restaurant, Bellanoes, she grinned from ear to ear. The first time he'd taken her there was for their one-year anniversary, and after that, they returned every year.

Which was why she looked at him now in surprise. "It's not our anniversary yet."

"Every day is an anniversary with you, my love," he said. "Besides, I felt that finally moving into our dream house deserved a proper celebration."

She was about to reply when the hostess approached to take them to their table, where Mason helped her settle into her seat.

Instantly, a waitress appeared to take their orders.

Mason eyed the young woman suspiciously. She was obviously new, and Mason wasn't fond of change. "Where is Mark?"

"He quit two months ago," the waitress replied, a bit startled.

Mason seemed displeased, and Ashlyn understood why. Mark was by far the best waiter who'd ever served them. It was like he could read their minds, and his suggestions were always spot-on.

Mason ordered for both of them.

As they waited for the food, they engaged in light chatter. Mason told her about his day, and how he had been offered another big job in San Francisco.

"I don't have the time for it, of course. I'm too busy locally as it is."

Part of Ashlyn was glad to hear that. She didn't like when he had to travel. It was depressing without him.

The waitress returned and started to put food on their table.

Mason eyed the steak with suspicion, picking up his knife and cutting into it. He flicked his gaze up to the waitress and a slight smile crossed his lips. "Perfect."

The waitress flushed and then lifted the wine bottle. "I

hope this wine meets with your approval as well," she murmured.

Mason gestured for her to pour him a sample and he swirled it in his glass, then sniffed it and took a sip. He made a face, as though something was off. "This does not. Do you have another selection?"

The waitress frowned. "One moment, sir. I'm sorry, I thought this was—" She waved her hand toward someone, and another waiter rushed over with a different bottle. Taking it, she looked at the label and nodded. "This one should pair better with your food, sir. I'm sorry." Again she poured a sample.

Mason did the same as before, but this time his smile returned. "This will do fine."

Ashlyn let out the breath she'd been holding. Mason was always a wine snob, and the staff at Bellanoes knew it. Even if this waitress was new, they would have made her aware of who he was and what was expected. Luckily, she hadn't screwed up too badly with the first choice.

"Is there anything else I can get for you?" she asked after pouring them each a glass.

"No, that will be all," Mason dismissed her. When she was gone, Mason looked across the table at Ashlyn and smiled. "I wanted this night to be perfect and for a moment there I was afraid she was going to ruin it."

Ashlyn took his offered hand across the table and squeezed his fingers. "Nothing could ruin tonight for me. I'm with you and that makes it perfect."

Mason raised her hand and kissed her knuckles. "I love you more than you will ever know."

"And I love you."

They enjoyed their meal, chatting about his current

design for one of his newest clients, and then Mason wiped his mouth and set his napkin down next to his plate. He smiled over at her again and said, "Excuse me, darling, I'm going to have a quick word with the chef."

Ashlyn nodded and picked up her wine as he stood. "Do tell him my steak was perfectly cooked and I quite enjoyed it."

Mason leaned down and kissed her cheek. "I will."

She watched him head toward the kitchen as she sipped her wine. It dawned on her that she was on her third glass and probably shouldn't drink any more. Mason didn't like when she was tipsy, so she did her best to always stay mostly sober. Setting the wine glass down, she switched to water.

While she waited, Ashlyn pulled her phone from her bag to check her messages. She was delighted to see that she'd had an email from a potential new client. She couldn't wait to tell Mason.

Looking up, she saw him returning, a smile on his face. She was sure his talk with the chef had gone well. "Guess what?" she murmured, excitement in her voice.

Mason retook his seat. "You love me and want to make love right here on this table?"

Ashlyn grinned. "I do love you, but no, not unless you've managed to buy this place and send everyone home." She laughed. "Did you?"

His eyes sparkled with laughter. "No, but give me a minute and I will."

Ashlyn shook her head, still laughing. "You're so silly."

"So what did you want me to guess?" he asked, lifting her hand and kissing her fingers.

"I have an email from a potential new client."

Mason's grin widened. "That's fantastic news, sweetheart. I suppose it's a good thing I spoke to the chef then."

"What? Why?" Ashlyn asked, confused.

"He's bringing out your favorite, crème brûlée."

Ashlyn couldn't help but think she'd married the perfect man and that this was the perfect night. If only that creepy feeling of being watched wasn't back in full force, she might have actually enjoyed that dessert.

4

A full month in her new home had passed, and things were going great. Mostly.

There were times when Mason returned from work moodier than usual, and would go to his man cave to blow off some steam. Although there was a perfectly good explanation for his behavior and mood swings, it was hard for her to see him like that.

But that was life. Good and bad. And this wasn't necessarily bad. Ashlyn was worried because he was always working so hard. He did it for her, though, so she could have this home and all the other conveniences.

She was sure that was why he'd accepted this big project from the city. He was building a new hospital, and a lot of people were involved, including politicians and investors. And that meant the media was all over it.

Mason hated when they called him for interviews. He did them because it was great exposure for his company and his brand, but it always left him in a bad mood since he was forced to do the whole dog-and-pony show.

Ashlyn was in the kitchen finishing dinner when she heard Mason coming into the house.

"I don't care if it's for a good cause. If they want me, then they have to pay my usual rates," Mason snapped, speaking on the phone. "I don't run a charity organization; it's a legitimate business," he added, walking into the kitchen.

Ashlyn smiled as he approached, trying to show support that even though he was having a rough day, she was there for him and loved him. But she was anxious that he had come home in such a bad mood, considering what she had to share. When she was growing up, her father tended to overreact when money was involved, so it was a knee-jerk reaction for her. Then again, there was a possibility that she was making a fuss out of nothing. Mason wasn't like her father.

There was a small pause in the conversation, as he listened to what the other party had to say, which he used to kiss her on the lips. His face softened for the tiniest of moments. Moving away, he frowned again. "Patrick, tell them there will be no negotiations."

Now she knew with whom he was speaking. Patrick Michelson was his lawyer.

Mason wrapped up his conversation with Patrick, carelessly throwing his phone onto the counter. "Sorry about that," he said, approaching her again. "Hello, my love," he said before kissing her again, greeting her the proper way.

"Problems?" she asked as they parted.

"Not really. The usual bullshit."

She nodded.

"What's that wonderful smell?" he asked, sniffing the air dramatically.

"Your favorite," she said, grinning.

He smiled. "I knew I did the right thing by marrying you."

"Of course you did," she replied.

"How was your day, apart from thinking about your husband?" he asked.

"A firm contacted me to do their office space."

"That's great news. What does that make, your eighth client now?"

"Yes. Sadly, the bad news is that when I wanted to go to town, my car broke down and I couldn't find anyone willing to come all the way here to check it out."

That wasn't 100 percent true. Some asked for incredible sums of money, and Ashlyn suspected it was because she was a woman. If Mason spoke with them, she was sure it would be a completely different situation.

"Why did you want to go to town?"

"To have a business meeting with the folks from that firm, and maybe visit my parents."

Mason opened the fridge to get a bottle of water. "Good thing it broke down here and not on the road. I would be worried sick."

She nodded. Though she was curious to know why it had broken down in the first place. It was a fairly new car.

"Do you have someone you can call to check it out for me?" she asked hopefully. "I don't know what's wrong with it."

"I can take a look at it, and if I can't fix it, then I can drive you wherever you want to go," he replied.

She gave him a look. "I'd love for you to look at it, but although I appreciate the offer, you're never here, so how would you have time to drive me around town?"

"I know my hours can get unpredictable, but I'm doing

my best to always be here for you," he replied, completely missing her point.

She raised her hands in supplication. "I wasn't trying to start an argument or complain about your work. I was pointing out how I need to be mobile. I need to be able to go to town, conduct business, and visit friends and family without having to call you or rely on you," she concluded, feeling slightly silly for having to say all that in the first place. It was so logical to her. Why wasn't it to him?

Mason sighed. "I'll look at the car. If I can't fix it, then we'll see about getting it to someone. I know you want to be able to pick up and go when you want, but honestly, I worry about you being on the road with all the lunatics. Can't you just do Zoom meetings with your clients? Then you wouldn't have to leave the house."

Ashlyn frowned. That wasn't the point. "I mean, yes, I could but—"

"And do you really have to go see your family so much? They always cause you so much drama."

"I know, but—"

"You've got your own life and career to focus on now. You don't need to be at their beck and call every second of the day trying to fix their problems."

Ashlyn knew that Mason didn't like how much time she'd spent "fixing" family issues, mostly brought on by Karina and her dirt-bag boyfriends. But they were still her family and she felt obligated to help when she could.

And then something else occurred to her. Discussing with him how important it was for her to see her family regularly was pointless because Mason had no contact with his own family. They were estranged, to put it mildly. The last time he'd seen them was right before he went to college.

And they were not invited to their wedding. Ashlyn had never met them.

She had no idea what happened between him and his parents because he never talked about it, but she knew it was something bad. Once, while slightly intoxicated, he commented how they'd abandoned him. She had no idea what that had actually meant, but her heart still broke seeing him in so much pain.

No wonder he was so clingy with her. He was afraid she would abandon him like his family had. So, she tried to show him that she was the only family he ever needed. Until they had children, naturally.

"I see your point," she replied eventually. "I would still like to have my car fixed. If you can't fix it, then I will find a mechanic," she said with finality, needing this conversation to end. It was obvious they were of a different opinion, and she didn't like that. She hated any kind of tension between them.

Mason glared at her and then strode toward the garage door and slammed it open. He was obviously angry, but she couldn't see why he was so mad at her. He returned a few minutes later, and said he couldn't fix the damn thing, then without another word yanked open the door to his man cave and disappeared.

She realized that Mason hadn't even bothered to actually look at it.

In the next couple of days, she found a mechanic, thanks to a little help from her father. He came to her home and checked out her car. As it turned out, it was an easy fix; it just needed a battery replacement and she was mobile once again in no time, which made her happy.

She was the only one. Mason definitely wasn't, once she informed him that her car had just needed a new battery.

She couldn't understand his behavior. "Is this about the money? Because the payment wasn't that costly."

He scoffed in return. "No. Of course it's not about money. I have enough money to buy you a hundred cars if that's what you want."

"Then what's the problem?" she pleaded. "I promise I will take good care of it. It won't break down again."

"The thought of you alone on the road, where a lot can happen, is driving me insane." Mason sighed. "It's just I saw a woman in a really bad accident on the way into the city the other day and she died. I just don't want to lose you."

"Mason, you can't protect me from everything, and you shouldn't have to. I know how to take care of myself. Nothing bad is going to happen to me."

Apparently, that was the worst thing she could've said because he waved his hand almost dismissively. "You don't understand. Just forget about it." And with that, he turned around and went to his man cave.

He needs some space to cool down.

He was right about one thing. Ashlyn understood nothing.

What just happened? How? Why were they arguing about her car in the first place? Nothing made sense to her anymore. And she couldn't stop stressing about all that was said. It bothered her that he'd behaved like that. It bothered her that he'd gotten upset, so she tried her best to find other ways to make him happy because it wasn't like she could get rid of her car. She needed it.

Nevertheless, she would definitely try to be a better wife,

make amends, and fix this ripple between them because ultimately, she loved him and knew he loved her as well. And that made all the difference in the world. It made her want to put in the effort.

5

Ashlyn was frustrated. Mason was still in a mood about her driving, and it was causing her to question herself and their relationship. It had been more than a week and he was still upset over it. Nothing she said seemed to bring him around.

It was no surprise to her that he had a controlling personality, partly because of his issues with his family, and partly because he was the head of a very successful business. Those kinds of personality traits—commanding, confident, domineering—came with the territory. Mason was used to people following his orders without questioning him.

However, she was not one of his employees. She was his wife, and although she recognized that he was under a lot of daily stress and tried her best to not be difficult and unreasonable, there were some things she just couldn't agree to.

Every time he brought up the safety of her driving on her own and she said she understood, but disagreed with him about it, he'd storm off to his man cave. She was starting to resent allowing him to have one. Because it felt like he was too dismissive of her and their relationship. He was acting like a child.

You're overreacting again. Spending all this time alone—always working for her business, or around the house—without socializing with other friends and family was starting to make her feel kind of crazy, over-analyzing things. It didn't help that Mason was always moody now when they were together.

She decided she was thinking too much. There was nothing wrong with her marriage. If things were a little bit off, that was because they were both under a lot of stress, constantly working. They needed a breather, which was precisely why she got super excited when her mom invited her and Mason to dinner on Sunday.

Sunday dinners at the Dawsons' house were important. It was always special no matter whether they were struggling financially. Ashlyn was excited to enjoy her mother's cooking, especially if she arrived while her mom was still at church and brought all the fresh groceries.

She could always say she craved a specific dish and had no idea whether her mom had all the ingredients to make it.

A plan formed inside her head as she told Mason that her mom had invited them to dinner the following night.

He was scrolling through his emails at the time, and without looking up, he said, "I'm not going."

His words really took her by surprise. Not to mention, it hurt her that he said that, as though there was no room for discussion. His mind was set.

"Why not?" she asked.

"I'm tired. I've had a long day and tomorrow will be a long one as well." Yes, he worked weekends as well. No rest for the workaholics. "I can't deal with your parents on top of everything. I moved us here so we wouldn't have to see them that often."

Ashlyn jerked as though she'd been hit but recovered quickly. The initial shock was replaced with anger. "What's so wrong with my parents that you had to run away from them?" She specifically phrased it like that knowing it would bother him.

She was right.

He made a face. "You know how they get around me."

Oh, so now it was *their* fault? "They love you, and you're not being fair."

Mason snorted. "Yeah, they love me. What a joke."

"They don't know you like I do, but that doesn't mean they are not fond of you," she tried to reassure him.

Mason worked long hours, and it was hard to arrange social gatherings, so Ashlyn tended to save Mason's free time for just the two of them. Maybe that was a mistake. Maybe if she forced both sides to spend a little more time together, they wouldn't end up in situations like this.

"Let's be honest. Your mother wishes you had married someone else, and your father doesn't trust me. And don't even get me started on that sister of yours."

"So now you have issues with Karina as well. Perfect."

"Don't play like that. You have issues with her, too."

"She's my sister," Ashlyn raised her voice. "She's had some issues, but that doesn't mean you can sit here and judge her."

Maybe that was one of the problems. Mason had told her that he was an only child to neglectful parents. Maybe he couldn't understand certain family dynamics because he hadn't experienced them.

"Oh please, Ashlyn. Don't get so overprotective, especially when she doesn't deserve it. You, better than anyone else, know what a trainwreck she is. You told me yourself how she stole money from you," he tossed in her face.

Ashlyn had told him that in confidence while heartbroken and emotional after a fight with her sister. "That was a long time ago," Ashlyn said calmly. It was an effort, yet she managed. "She's changed since then. Gotten her life back on track." And that was no lie. She believed it.

Mason looked at her, completely unimpressed, which pissed her off even more.

She was done with this conversation. "You know what? You're absolutely right. If you feel like that toward my family, then you shouldn't go." She was done trying to coddle him about it. She was done arguing. Maybe she needed time away from him.

Mason nodded as though what she'd said made perfect sense. His whole face was screaming *finally*, which made her grit her teeth.

"Thank you, my love, for understanding. Trust me, we will have a much better time staying home, just the two of us. We can order something to eat, and we can even watch that TV show you love so much."

He was talking about *Game of Thrones*, which she'd begged him to watch with her for months and he always found excuses not to. And it irked her that he dangled that in front of her now, like a carrot on a stick, to have his way.

"Oh, I'm sorry, you misunderstood. I'm still going."

She could see all kinds of emotions pass over his face.

"But you're more than welcome to make a night out of it on your own. Watch the show. It's great," she added for good measure.

"Ashlyn—"

"*Don't*, Mason," she interrupted. "I've heard enough." And this time around, it was she who left him standing there.

She worked until late that night. Perhaps a part of her was avoiding him, knowing that if he apologized, she would waver. The rest was still reeling. Everything he'd said had hurt her feelings. He thought so poorly of her family.

Does he think the same about me? She banished that thought immediately. She was tired. That was the reason her thoughts were all over the place.

Arriving in their bedroom, she found it empty.

Why did she feel like part of her heart, her soul, was missing?

The next morning, Mason was nowhere to be found.

She was frustrated as hell that he had reacted the way he had. At the same time, had she overreacted? She didn't think so.

The whole situation, the unexpected fight, saddened her as well. It was sad that people in her life—the people she cared about the most—couldn't get along.

She left the house alone and stopped at the market to buy food for her family. As she shopped, she once again had that feeling of being watched. It was very eerie and had her looking over her shoulder as she moved down the aisle. It seemed like every time she came into town, she got this feeling, and it was really starting to get to her.

Hurrying through the shopping, she paid for it all and then rushed out to her car, quickly loading it up and putting the cart away. The feeling of being observed didn't go away until she reached her parents' neighborhood.

Her parents' house was empty when she arrived, which meant her mother had convinced the entire household to go with her to the church service. She would probably nag because Ashlyn wasn't there as well. Although her mother was very religious and Ashlyn had been raised to go to church, she realized over time that it wasn't for her. She believed in God, but she didn't necessarily believe in the church.

After putting all the food she bought in the fridge and cupboards, she settled in to wait for her family. Glancing about at her father's makeshift office in the corner, she was horrified to find that Karina hadn't been joking: Some of the components were actually duct-taped. Only her father would do something like that.

She would definitely buy him a new computer and install it while he wasn't home, including moving all the files he'd need for work, and then throw away that old piece of trash. That way, there would be nothing he could do about it.

She didn't have to wait too long for her family to return home. They were pleasantly surprised to find her there already.

Naturally, her mother knew something was bothering her the instant she stepped inside. "Where is Mason?" she asked after they'd all greeted one another.

"He couldn't come. Work," Ashlyn replied, hoping that would be the end of it.

She wasn't that lucky.

"There's no need for you to cover for him. I know he didn't want to come."

Was it so obvious to all of them that they couldn't be in the same room with each other, apart from her? The notion was as sobering as it was devastating. How could she have been so blind? Then something else occurred to her. If she had failed to see this, what else had flown under her radar?

"Is that true?" Karina wondered, and there was genuine excitement in her voice that Ashlyn resented, so she didn't answer. "Maybe it's better this way. He always looked down on us, like a snob," Karina continued.

"Don't speak about my husband like that," Ashlyn snapped.

She had hoped for a nice afternoon with her family, yet there they were, arguing. It was as though she was stuck in a loop and couldn't get out, no matter how much she tried.

Was she the problem?

Karina rolled her eyes. "And how should I speak about him? He's never around, so what else am I supposed to think?"

"Can't you just be happy for me?" Ashlyn said, getting tired. Tired of arguing, of drama.

"Are you?" Karina countered.

"Excuse me?"

"Are you happy?"

"Of course I am," Ashlyn countered immediately.

Karina nodded. "Yeah, tell that to your face."

"Karina, just stop."

"All I'm saying is that if you're not happy, just divorce his ass—and make sure to take half of his money. You deserve it."

"What are you talking about? I'm not getting a divorce," Ashlyn said, raising her voice.

"Honey, don't get angry at your sister," her mother said. "We only want what's best for you."

"Everything is fine, Mom. Mason and I are fine."

"Fine usually means the opposite," Karina commented,

and her mom sent her a look, so she raised her hands in surrender. "I'm just saying."

Ashlyn sighed. "I'm not in denial. Mason and I have a very good marriage, but there has been tension lately. We argue constantly over the most idiotic things. However, I'm sure those are temporary problems."

None of them looked convinced by what she was saying. And the most tragic part was that neither was she. *What if Mason is right? Not about my family but about me being out on my own?* she thought as her mind drifted back to the creepy feeling she'd had while shopping. *What if he's just trying to protect me?* Ashlyn frowned. This wasn't the time to be thinking about that.

"Anyway," she said to distract herself from the surge of thoughts coming her way. "What are we cooking today?"

Apparently, her mom decided to take pity on her because she allowed the change of subject, and then all was forgotten when she discovered Ashlyn had restocked the fridge.

Despite that emotional and somewhat painful start, Ashlyn spent a nice day with her family. It felt like old times, with Mom fussing in the kitchen while their dad watched some random game, yelling at the referees that they were blind, corrupt, and so on.

Once she returned home, she discovered Mason had installed a security system on the house. It was blaring as soon as she unlocked the front door. *What the hell?*

Not surprisingly, she found him in his office. "Mason, what's this?" She put her hands over her ears trying to block the loud alarm.

"It's an alarm system."

"Great, but why do we have it in the first place?" she

wondered as she followed him to the keypad where he punched in a code.

"I've been meaning to put one in for quite some time, and since I had time today, I took care of it," he replied, returning to his office. He began shuffling some papers, almost ignoring her.

He still refused to look at her. He hadn't even glanced at her, not once. And the lack of a proper greeting was notable as well.

"Why do we need an alarm system?" she insisted.

"We just do. It's for safety," he replied sternly.

It was obvious he was still angry with her for leaving to have dinner with her family. *He* was angry? After all he'd said?

That made her level of anger rise again, and she did her best to force it back down.

"Fine. Whatever," she replied eventually.

Since he'd chosen to act like that, she let him be and went to her office, despite feeling that his behavior was rude and wondering why he'd installed something that really wasn't necessary.

She was sure he would speak to her once he calmed down. This wasn't their first fight, and as it looked, it definitely wouldn't be the last.

That was depressing as hell.

Midway to her office, she realized she had no desire to work, so instead, she went to the bedroom and went to sleep.

Some days are better put behind as soon as possible, anyway.

6

Two days had passed since Ashlyn and Mason got into a fight over her family. And eventually things did calm down. Ashlyn knew he was feeling sorry. It was obvious in everything he did, the flowers he was sending, but especially in the fact that he was coming home earlier, and he finally apologized.

They were watching television together, a rare treat in which Mason indulged her by pretending to be interested in the music show she liked. Ashlyn was lying happily on Mason's shoulder, finally feeling like things between them were brightening up. Why would he go through this obvious torture if he didn't care anymore?

About halfway through, the program stopped for some commercials and short news.

According to the news reporter, nothing good had happened in the state in the last twenty-four hours. It was all about car crashes, murders, deaths, and other accidents. They, as a society, were fascinated by the macabre.

Tired of hearing such glum reports, Ashlyn was about to

change the program when a news alert on the screen stopped her.

"Two nights ago, Olga Weathers was grabbed off the streets in Tahoe in a bizarre kidnapping. As you can see on the footage, an unidentified man grabbed her and drove away in an unmarked delivery van. She is the third woman from this area to be abducted in the past nine months."

"This is the third kidnapping? How haven't I heard of this before now?" Ashlyn said with a shake of her head.

The reporter asked people on the street why something like that had happened. Some blamed mobsters and human traffickers, and others blamed a serial killer.

At the words *serial killer*, a shiver went down her spine, and it was for two very selfish reasons. First, the kidnapped young woman had green eyes and distinctive red hair. Although nobody could mistake them as twins, they definitely shared all the same traits. And that filled her with uneasiness. Second was the fact that over the past several months, every time she'd gone into the city, she'd felt like someone was watching her, following her. Was it this serial killer?

Mason put a hand over her shoulder, comfortingly, protectively, and she snuggled even closer to him.

"This is why I'm glad we are no longer in the city," he commented.

It wasn't like they lived in New York City or Los Angeles. The city was small in comparison and nestled next to a very famous tourist-adored lake. Besides, the problem wasn't geography. It was the predator in it.

"It's not the city's fault there's crime. It's people's fault," Ashlyn pointed out. "Some people are just born evil and sick, and it's society's job to stop them in time."

grabbed her Stanley cup from the night table and took a drink of water.

"Go back to sleep, my love," he replied, reaching down, and stroking her hair. "I didn't mean to wake you with my insomnia."

Ashlyn closed her eyes and drifted back to sleep, but it certainly wasn't restful.

In the morning, she couldn't shake all the weird dreams she'd had. It was hard to choose which one had disturbed her the most.

It bothered her that she was so stressed about the state of her relationship with Mason that she'd started to dream about such distressing things.

Her stomach did a little flip as she braced herself to enter the kitchen and encounter Mason.

Pure relief washed over her when he turned from the stove and smiled at her. He looked beyond cheerful as he prepared breakfast. Mason rarely cooked, but when he did it was to prepare her favorite pancakes. That warmed her heart because it showed her that he was bothered by their argument.

After kissing her a little longer and a little more passionately than as of late, Mason ushered her to a seat at the table and served her a plate of pancakes with maple syrup and a cup of coffee.

A few minutes later, he left for work, promising he would be back early so they could spend some time together.

A slight bite on her lower lip painted a pretty clear picture of what was on his mind, and perhaps he was right, and this could be fixed with a lot of sex. They were both stressed, and being intimate could help with that.

And then everything would return to normal.

What was happening with him lately? Was it a midlife crisis? She hoped not. Mason was only forty.

Besides, didn't a mid-life crisis include divorce and finding a much younger wife? She dismissed the thought. Mason would never do something like that. He loved her. She knew that with her whole heart.

Then again, she couldn't believe the things that left his mouth lately. Was that really how he thought? Was that the man she'd married?

Perhaps Mason had more things in common with her father than she cared to admit and now could not ignore. He, too, believed women had to know their place, and it was troubling, to say the least, that Mason showed similar traits. He hadn't been like this before. Or had he, and she'd failed to notice? That thought frightened her.

Feeling beyond sad and not to mention confused about how they'd gotten to the point where they couldn't even watch TV together without arguing and his practically avoiding her at every turn and hiding in his cave, she turned the TV off and went to the bedroom.

She knew better than to wait for him to come to bed, so she stripped into her nightgown, one that Mason liked the best and always complimented her on how pure yet sexy she looked in it, and cried herself to sleep.

Nightmares about her and Mason made her slumber restless.

Some time, in the middle of the night, trying to escape a dream of her crying as Mason was kissing another woman, Ashlyn opened her eyes to see her husband standing over her, just watching her.

"Mason?" she murmured looking up at him as she

"What are you doing?"

"I don't want to argue with you about this. Can't you see this is a safety issue?" He pursed his lips and stared at the TV. "She never should have been out there on the street like that. It was asking for trouble, and if you can't see that, then I can't be around you right now." He sounded upset and almost hurt that she didn't agree with him.

Ashlyn thought he was the one being unreasonable despite the fact that she'd felt a lot of apprehension lately when going about her business in town. She wasn't about to admit to him that she felt unsafe in the city though. "Mason, sit back down," she pleaded. "We were watching TV together."

"I'm not in the mood anymore." He sighed and left the living room, leaving her alone.

Ashlyn was shocked that he'd abandoned her and their precious time together. *Was this an excuse to go and play video games in his man cave? Does he just not want to spend time with me?*

Unbelievable.

That was his M.O. as of late. Each time he was displeased about anything, he just turned around and went away.

Does he have a gaming addiction? she wondered. Mason was too serious for something like that, though. He wouldn't allow himself to get addicted, although he'd played a lot lately. Perhaps it was a temporary fascination. He worked too hard. He deserved to relax in any way he wanted.

Realizing she was defending him made her stop.

You're angry at him, remember? Shortly after his retreat, she could hear music playing and some kind of strange banging coming from his man cave.

"True," Mason allowed. "Although, it's possible the woman might also have some blame too."

Ashlyn rose so she could look into her husband's face. "Excuse me?" Was he victim-blaming? Would he blame her if she were the one kidnapped?

"Well, she was alone on the street at night. That's asking for trouble if you ask me," he concluded with a small shrug.

Her heart raced. She knew it could just have easily been her, considering the weird feelings of being stalked she'd had while in the city. "I can't believe you would think that's a reason to blame her for her own abduction." Ashlyn was flabbergasted.

"Why?" He seemed genuinely confused that Ashlyn was disagreeing with him.

"Mason, you're blaming the victim for what happened to her," Ashlyn countered, raising her voice. "If a man had been kidnapped, would you blame him for being out on the street at night alone?"

"No, because he's a man and that wouldn't happen."

"So just because she's a woman she shouldn't be able to go where she pleases, whenever she pleases, without having an army protecting her?"

"You're being naive, Ashlyn. There are monsters in this world, ones who prey on women," Mason reprimanded.

"Maybe so. But that doesn't mean you're right. Her being kidnapped isn't her fault. It's that psycho's fault who dared to think he was entitled to abduct her. And he should be caught and locked up for what he did. Anyone who thinks he's better than someone else and can torment another human being deserves to be punished in the worst possible way."

Mason got up.

7

Be patient, Ashlyn advised herself. Her mother always told her that women had to be patient with their husbands because they were nothing but big children. And she was honestly trying. Yet as it turned out, patience wasn't one of her virtues.

Perhaps that was why her name was Ashlyn and not Patience. Chuckling at her bad joke, she returned to the matter at hand.

Ashlyn could no longer ignore the signs. Something was broken in her marriage. Although she tried not to point fingers, it was clear that Mason was the driving force behind many of their arguments. Things he said about her family and some of his points of view were hurtful and alarming.

She was trying her best to make amends, to correct whatever was wrong, but it made no difference because Mason was not meeting her halfway. She even stopped mentioning her family so as to not make him angry, and he acted as though he didn't seem to notice her efforts.

No, that wasn't completely true, part of her rebelled. It

was more like he acted as though all her efforts were nothing special to begin with. As though that type of behavior was expected of her by default. It was not witnessed as a display of goodwill on her part, something that would make their marriage harmonious again. And that was the true cause of her anguish. His lack of appreciation was infuriating.

It was downright insulting that he saw all she was doing as normal and expected, while on the other hand, he remained completely oblivious about his mistakes and contribution to the marital problems.

Was that ignorance or arrogance?

Either way, Mason refused to take any kind of responsibility for his part in their damaged romance. He was perfectly content to pretend all was well, but she wasn't. She couldn't live like that.

She couldn't tell how they'd started to rip apart or why it had happened in the first place, but she knew with almost surgical precision when it all started.

The problems had started when they moved to their dream house, which baffled her on so many levels. This was supposed to be the happiest chapter of their lives, during which they would finally start working on expanding their family. But instead, they constantly fought and couldn't agree completely on anything.

She couldn't understand why he'd changed so much since coming here. Did he perhaps have second thoughts about them, and this was his subconscious manner of trying to drive her away because he was too weak to break up with her on his own?

Ashlyn couldn't stop stressing, her mind coming up with all kinds of theories and scenarios.

Maybe he was having an affair, and his guilty conscience

was driving a wedge between them? She banished that since their sex life remained the same. That was the only thing that hadn't changed throughout this madness.

Was it possible she was finally coming down from cloud nine and seeing the man she married as he really was for the first time? That thought deeply disturbed her. On one hand, she refused to believe she had been that blind all these years. On the other, it would explain why her family had never been fond of her husband.

Even if that were true, the question remained... why now? What changed, and why did it change? Why had her perspective changed so much?

Ashlyn had so many questions, but failed to see the answers. She didn't even know how to start seeking them. In other words, she felt utterly stuck.

She still loved her husband very much and, in her heart, knew he loved her as well, but she was miserable, and that was no way to live.

Regardless of the reasoning behind their marital problems, it all culminated during dinner one night. The TV was on, and Ashlyn and Mason could hear the news in the background as they ate. Mason liked to stay up to date with current affairs, although Ashlyn preferred music or something else a bit more cheerful. She was stressed enough, and all the doom and gloom the reporter talked about didn't help with her mood one bit.

The breaking news was that one of the biggest movie star couples were divorcing because of allegations that the husband had been cheating on his wife of six years with one of his co-stars.

The wife, who was just as big of a star as her husband, was speaking out and spilling all the details of their private life. She talked about how he had verbally abused her for years and had tried to undermine her and get her to turn down certain movie roles and all the while he'd been working to get his mistress bigger and better roles, roles that the wife was up for. She spoke of how controlling and manipulating he was and how he'd tried to isolate her from her friends and family.

"Poor woman," Ashlyn commented as they ate. "How could he do that to her?"

"I hate to say it, sweetheart, but she's probably lying. She's an actress after all. The bigger the scandal she can make of his infidelity the more money she'll probably get in the divorce."

Ashlyn couldn't believe that was his take on it. "Are you kidding me? He's done all that stuff to her. She has proof."

"We weren't there in the marriage with them. For all we know it's just movie magic. It's possible she cheated on him first and that's why he tried to keep her from certain roles and away from people who influenced her. That's what these Hollywood types do."

Ashlyn felt sick to her stomach. How could he hear what the actress described and think that? "He's the one who was cheating and abusing her. Not to mention gaslighting her. There is never a reason to keep a woman from her friends and family. How can you even think like that?"

"He's her husband. He probably knows more about the situation than we do," he said dismissively. "He's probably trying to protect her from her own self-destructive behaviors. That's what a good husband does."

She couldn't believe that was what he thought about the couple's situation. She had to wonder if that was what Mason was trying to do to her. Claiming he was trying to protect her by not wanting her to drive or see her family. "If that's the way you actually feel... I don't think—" She stopped and pushed her plate away, standing up.

Mason looked startled. "We're just having a conversation. I don't understand why you're getting so upset. I'm just sharing my thoughts on their situation."

Ashlyn didn't want to hear it. "Well, I'm glad I finally know your thoughts about how unequal men and women are. Is that what you're doing? Do you have a mistress too?" she practically yelled.

He got up from the table too, visibly rattled now, if not angered. "Don't speak like that," he snapped. "Why would you say something like that?"

"Would you tell me if you did?" she insisted.

Mason opened his mouth as though to say something then closed it, as though reconsidering. "I guess it depends on the situation," he eventually said.

Ashlyn felt like part of her heart just got cut out and had shriveled away. Without a word, she turned to leave the dining room.

Mason stopped her. He hugged her from behind, preventing her from leaving. "Ashlyn, calm down. You're blowing things out of proportion."

His words only infuriated her further. "I'm not the unreasonable one here. You're literally telling me you have a mistress, and I can't stand it. It's breaking my heart."

"You're putting words in my mouth. I never said that. I never even implied that." He sounded upset, but she figured he was just mad she was calling him out on his shit.

"No, you said that's what husbands do, which you are one. You excused his behavior and dismissed my feelings about it, and you didn't outright deny having one."

And saying that, she broke out of his embrace and left the room. He didn't follow her, and she was relieved. Slamming the door of their bedroom, Ashlyn completely fell apart, falling onto the bed.

Burying her head in the pillow, she screamed out of desperation, and cried her eyes out.

Had that just happened? Was he actually cheating on her?

Ashlyn was so upset by what he'd said and what he hadn't said. She had no idea where to go from here. Should she even stay with him? Remembering his heartless words, she wondered if she should even bother in the first place.

8

Ashlyn felt trapped between the Mason she'd known and loved for five years and the Mason she was getting to know. And she was definitely starting to resent their dream home for her problems because their life had been nearly perfect in the duplex. It all went downhill after relocating to this house in the middle of nowhere.

Damned house.

She had to admit she was not a huge fan of the man Mason had changed into. Especially since some of his statements were deeply disturbing to her.

Ashlyn was certain that something must have happened for him to act like this, to say the things he'd been saying lately. Had his mother hurt him so much all those years ago that he was just now starting to resent all women? Was that something that could happen? Or was something else going on? Was it this new mistress of his putting ideas into his head? Did he really hate women so much? If he did, why was he even with her?

She had no idea. All the same, she couldn't picture him as a woman hater because he had always been so kind, gentle, and full of love toward her. Maybe he had developed brain damage or cancer that was changing his personality. That wasn't the most comforting thought, but it was still a possible reason. A tumor could do that, right?

She was determined to find the root of the problems and try to fix their marriage. But she couldn't fix everything on her own no matter how much she tried. Mason had to want that as well, but she wasn't even sure he was aware there were problems.

He must know. They were not the same with each other as before. They fought constantly.

What if he doesn't care about me anymore? What if he really does have a mistress? Those thoughts were too hard to contemplate.

They wouldn't still be married if he didn't love her anymore. No matter his feelings for her, Mason was also a very pragmatic man. If he deemed them broken, he would have no problem ending it.

Surprisingly, Ashlyn found a sliver of comfort in that. There was still hope.

Then again, what if he wants to divorce me and is waiting for the best moment to present me with the papers? Thinking about that, her heart started to race. *What if he doesn't love me anymore? What if he doesn't want me anymore?*

Why was there no air in her office?

He was acting coldly. And he wouldn't have said all those things if he cared about her feelings.

Mason will divorce me. She forced herself to stop there because her spiraling thoughts were causing a panic attack.

This was just a bump in the road. Nothing major was going on in her life, in their marriage. They were both very stressed, and she was blowing things out of proportion.

All couples went through difficult stages. This was theirs. They would survive it, she was certain of that, especially with some professional help. She was sure couples' therapy would help them find their way back to each other, making them even stronger than before.

With her mind pretty much set on the next logical course of action, all that was left was to share her thoughts with Mason. And it saddened her that she wasn't looking forward to speaking with him about it. At the same time, that only strengthened her resolve because right there was a true testament to the state of their relationship.

Ever since that fight, they had steered clear of each other. He left for work before she awoke in the morning, and she made a point to work late before going to bed.

Living like that was depressing as hell.

She had to do this because there was now this constant tension when the two of them were in the same room. Bad things could happen as well, wrong things could be said, and that had to change if this marriage had any chance of surviving.

Reaching his study, she took a deep breath before knocking and going inside.

"We need to talk, Mason," she said with determination, with the confidence she didn't necessarily possess.

"Certainly, my love. What's the problem?" Although he said all the right things, the tone was off.

You're the problem, she wanted to say but couldn't.

Despite his lack of interest, Ashlyn pressed forward.

There was no going back now. "We are the problem, Mason. Our relationship."

He looked at her. "Excuse me?"

"You can't tell me you haven't noticed that we've been arguing a lot more since coming here."

"Of course I've noticed. But..." he started then apparently bit his tongue.

You thought it was the hysterical me causing all the drama? It was on the tip of her tongue, but she managed to rein in her temper.

Be part of the solution, not the problem.

"This situation is making me miserable, Mason, and I don't know how much more I can take." There. She'd said it.

"What are you saying?" he asked wide-eyed, going slightly pale. "You want to leave me?"

Mason looked genuinely alarmed by the prospect of that, and perhaps it was wrong of her, but it gave her some comfort. He still cared.

Ashlyn sighed. This was very difficult for her since she detested confrontations and arguments in general, but it had to be done for the greater good, for the prospect of a future together. "No, I don't want to leave. I want to be with you, but something is clearly wrong and I'm at the end of my rope. I think we need to go to couples' therapy."

He rose to stand next to her. Taking her hands in his, he kissed her knuckles. "Ashlyn, my love, it saddens me to hear you speak like this. I had no idea you've been feeling like that."

"That's my point. We haven't been able to speak with one another without arguing. We haven't been right for a while."

"I know," he agreed with a nod. "And it's my fault. I've been working too hard."

"It's not just that. Even when you're here, you're agitated, arguing, and then retreating to your man cave without resolving anything," she pointed out.

"I needed some time alone to process things."

"That's not the problem. Our being together, always fighting, is."

"I hear what you're saying. We need to spend some quality time together, just the two of us, to reconnect away from our everyday lives."

What? That wasn't at all where she'd thought this conversation would go. "What are you saying, Mason?"

"How about we take a week-long vacation?" he suggested. "A second honeymoon."

And that completely stunned her. "Can you do that?" Ashlyn knew how hectic his days at the office were because of the newest project.

"I can do whatever I want. It's my firm. Besides, I would do anything to make you happy. You know that, right?"

"Where would we even go?"

He thought about that for a moment. "How about New Orleans?"

On one hand, Ashlyn had always wanted to go there and was touched that Mason suggested it because it showed her that he was willing to do the work to make their marriage more harmonious.

On the other hand, she didn't fail to notice how he didn't actually say yes to seeing a therapist. Nevertheless, it was a step in the right direction. And she agreed with him. They needed some time away from work and all the stress of their everyday lives.

That was why she said, "Yes, I would love to go."

"Perfect," he said, kissing her on the mouth. "I'll start making preparations immediately."

She smiled. His suggestion of this trip warmed her heart. *This is going to work. We will work. We have to.*

9

Mason was super excited as he planned their second honeymoon, and Ashlyn had to admit his sudden good mood was contagious. After they agreed to leave town for a whole week, she found herself breathing lightly.

She did not foolishly believe this magic trip would solve all their marital problems, but it was definitely a step in the right direction. The atmosphere and the energy around the house shifted after their talk. There was no more tension between them, and they didn't have a single fight. Part of Ashlyn began to think that she'd exaggerated the whole thing. They'd fought, and Mason had said some things, but she was sure he hadn't actually meant them. It was stress combined with exhaustion. Going away for a while would fix that.

Ashlyn was particularly happy that Mason spent less time in his man cave as of late. He preferred spending time with her than playing video games.

Her thoughts were interrupted by Mason calling out to

her. They were researching New Orleans in his study. Mason was behind his computer as Ashlyn surfed on her phone.

"Honey, what was that restaurant's name you mentioned before?" he asked with a slight frown.

She replied instantly. Ashlyn had read about that magical spot in a book and immediately went to verify whether it was a real place. Her excitement had no boundaries when she discovered that it was. That was when she promised herself that she would definitely see it for herself.

"Why do you ask?" Ashlyn wondered, trying not to get excited. The waiting list for that place was insane, so it was prudent not to get her hopes up.

Although going by the number of butterflies in her stomach, it was quite possible that it was already too late.

"I want to make reservations."

Ashlyn was genuinely touched. The fact that he'd remembered that was the place she wanted to visit the most, after mentioning it only once, showed her how committed he was to her.

And then she processed what he said. "*Reservations*, as in plural?"

He nodded.

Oh, my God. Dining there once would be a dream come true. Visiting it again would be the next level.

Without being able to help herself, Ashlyn jumped from her seat and went to give Mason a kiss. He responded by wrapping his arms around her waist, pushing her to sit on his lap.

She could see all kinds of guides and traveling sites on his screen.

"Is there something else you have planned?" she asked,

mostly joking as he turned off the screen as though he didn't want her seeing too much.

"Of course. However, most are a surprise," he said.

"All I need is you," she replied honestly, giving him another kiss.

"And I need you, my love. But I still want you to experience New Orleans to its fullest and enjoy yourself. You've been waiting a long time to visit, and I want to give you everything."

"What about you?"

"As long as you're happy, I'm happy," he replied with a small shrug.

It was rare to see him so open and vulnerable.

Oh, Mason.

They kissed again, which led to other fun things.

It was no secret that Ashlyn was really looking forward to this vacation. They definitely deserved it. They hadn't traveled since they'd gotten married, and back then, they spent a whole month in Hawaii and its surrounding islands.

Occasionally Mason surprised her with a getaway weekend, but those were mostly work-related, so they didn't count. This trip to New Orleans would be different. It would be no work and all play.

As much as she could gather, since he was so tight-lipped about the whole trip, he'd planned a lot of fun activities. But not too many. She knew there would be time for romance because Mason sent her a dozen sets of sexy lingerie. She got hot and bothered trying them all on, picturing how Mason would react upon seeing her in them. It was understood that she packed everything.

Each day until the trip, Ashlyn caught herself fantasizing

about it. And the best part was that Mason was equally invested.

Driving into the city before the trip to pick up a few new outfits, Ashlyn found herself getting more and more excited. As she entered the dress shop, the hair on the back of her neck rose and she spun around to look out at the street. Someone was watching her again.

She looked up and down the street, taking in every person who passed by, but not one met her gaze. She couldn't figure out where the feeling was coming from. It didn't make any sense. Feeling uneasy, she moved more fully into the shop and did her shopping.

Once she was done, she slipped back outside and stood on the sidewalk waiting for the feeling to appear again, but it didn't.

Relieved, Ashlyn decided to pay her family a visit since she wouldn't be able to see them before she and Mason left for their trip.

"I'm very excited, and Mason is too," she told them. "He's constantly sending me pictures of places we have to visit, restaurant menus with highlighted foods we have to try, and so on. He's like a kid."

"I'm very happy for you, honey," her mother said, offering a small smile.

Her father remained composed as he offered his two cents. "It's good he finally pulled his head out of his ass. A happy wife means a happy life."

Ashlyn suppressed an eye roll.

The only person who remained silent, as though not impressed with what she shared, was Karina. It bugged Ashlyn to no end.

"What? Nothing to say?"

Ashlyn expected that Karina would offer her apologies, say she'd been wrong to judge Mason so harshly, and to assume their marriage was in crisis when it clearly wasn't. As it turned out, that was too much to ask from her younger sister.

"Oh, I have plenty to say," she said. "I just don't think you'll like it."

"Karina," her mother warned.

"No, Mom, let her speak," Ashlyn interjected. "Come on, Karina, try me."

Karina shrugged as though to say *you asked for it*. "Based on all you said, it's clear to me how he managed to manipulate you."

"Excuse me?"

"Mason successfully dodged going to therapy, like you initially wanted, instead dazzling you with this trip that you didn't want."

"It's nothing like that," Ashlyn countered, getting instantly flustered. "We need a break."

"From what?"

"From work. From everything. And besides, I don't believe this to be a magical trip, but a step in the right direction," Ashlyn said indignantly.

"So he agreed to therapy?" Karina pressed.

She had her there. "Well, not yet. However, I'm sure that's on the agenda when we return from New Orleans. Mason is just too busy now planning this trip for us. I don't want to burden him further."

Karina made a face. "You're constantly making excuses for him. Can't you see that?"

"And you're intentionally trying to provoke me, but you know what? I'm done arguing with you."

"No one is arguing."

"Yes, you are. I came here to share some good news, share how happy I am after feeling like something was wrong in my marriage, and you can't handle it. Well, sorry, Karina. I'm not responsible that you're not content with your life. If you can't be there for me like a sister should, then that's your problem, not mine." And with that, she left.

Ashlyn could hear her mother calling after her, pleading with her to return, but she was done.

Perhaps Mason was right. Something was wrong with her family, she thought as she drove home.

Unfortunately, as she drove, she couldn't shake the feeling that she was being followed and she couldn't help but wonder what they were after.

10

Two days before their big trip to New Orleans, Mason spent the night in Tahoe, making sure everything at his firm would run smoothly in his absence.

It was a small price to pay, because she would soon have him all to herself for a week. She had no problems with him staying in the city. It wouldn't be the first time. Although he traveled less as of late, Ashlyn was used to spending a few nights alone.

This was the first time in this new house, but she would manage. Actually, she caught herself feeling relieved to spend the night alone, away from her husband, and that somewhat alarmed her.

That was not a feeling she wanted or needed right before going with him on a second honeymoon.

Ashlyn chalked up her feelings to nervousness. This trip represented reconnection and rekindled intimacy, and that could be scary, especially if she was putting a lot of pressure on herself for everything to be perfect.

At the same time, she was looking forward to it. It was a dream come true.

You're all over the place, she chided herself, preparing for bed.

As she tried to sleep, she heard muffled sounds coming from somewhere in the house.

You're hearing things, she reassured herself, trying to relax. But the noises persisted, making her open her eyes to the pitch darkness. She preferred to sleep in it, yet now, being all alone in the middle of the woods, her mother's fears came to taunt her. Was it that presence that had been following her in the city? The one she'd done her best to lose the other day before coming home? Had whoever it was figured out where she lived? Had they broken in?

You're not afraid, she told herself.

"Mason?" she called out. Perhaps he'd reconsidered and decided to come home.

No one replied.

Of course it wasn't Mason. She felt ridiculous for thinking that for even a second.

It couldn't have been him. She hadn't heard his car. In fact, she hadn't heard any car, and besides, if he said he was pulling an all-nighter, then that was exactly what he would do. He was strict in that regard. He wouldn't change his mind no matter how tired he got.

Sadly, that didn't help her one bit because she could still definitely hear something. Getting out of bed, Ashlyn went to investigate.

This is how a lot of horror movies start, she thought and instantly regretted it.

I will not get murdered in my own home, she thought, yet just to be on the safe side, she grabbed the first thing in reach, a small vase, currently empty, and carried it as she descended the stairs.

Walking through the ground floor, she couldn't pinpoint the sounds. She couldn't even decipher what they were to begin with.

What is that? she asked out of frustration. She didn't feel scared anymore, just curious and slightly frustrated.

Are there raccoons? That made her pause and concentrate on the sound. *Maybe.* Although at the same time, it was kind of far-fetched since the house was surrounded by such a high fence, but that didn't mean raccoons wouldn't find a way over it. They were highly intelligent and resourceful.

Reaching the kitchen door that led to the backyard, she realized she wasn't brave enough to go outside and test her theory.

So, she just stood there with a vase in her hands. Eventually, the noises stopped, and relieved, Ashlyn returned to bed.

That was weird. She felt slightly nervous sleeping alone now and couldn't wait for her husband to return in the early hours.

Then again, this whole thing might have happened because she was all alone, and fear could make people exaggerate.

Either way, she had trouble falling asleep and was more than relieved, even happy, when the next time she opened her eyes, Mason was in bed beside her.

11

New Orleans was even better than her wildest dreams. There were no words to describe how Ashlyn felt walking those streets. It was such a colorful city, with beautiful people, and all the pictures she'd seen did not do it justice.

Although it wasn't Mardi Gras, they still got to experience a taste of it all on Bourbon Street. Ashlyn was enamored. However, there was a possibility she felt like that because of her company. Mason was different there. At first it was jarring to see her husband more relaxed and to have him all to herself all day, every day. It was such a huge contrast from their life back home. She cherished each second spent with Mason in New Orleans. Most of all, she cherished how attentive he was.

Soon she was reminded why she'd fallen in love with her husband in the first place. With Mason's help, Ashlyn managed to relax and fully experience this great adventure, not only the city but her marriage as well.

Now she couldn't understand why she'd made such a big

fuss in the first place. Mason was still the man she'd married all those years ago, the one she deeply loved and respected. And now more than ever, she was convinced that this was the man she wanted to spend her life with, have children with, and grow old with.

What she liked most about the city were the people and their attitude toward life. They understood how precious life was, and they savored it. That way of thinking was embedded in every aspect of life, especially in the food. Ashlyn was of the mind that everyone should think more like that. That was why she allowed herself to let go and indulge.

Ashlyn ate so much of the delicious local food—gumbo, crawfish etouffee, and jambalaya—that she started to worry she'd gain weight. She couldn't help herself. The smells around her were so mouthwatering and inviting that there was no escaping indulging. And don't get her started on all the sweets. They were her kryptonite.

Luckily, Mason didn't seem to mind if she put on an extra pound. He acted completely insatiable with her. He looked at her constantly, as though he couldn't wait to have her all to himself back in the room. It was thrilling. Their sex life had never been better.

"Ready for another muffuletta?" Mason asked her as they sat in a restaurant overlooking Lake Pontchartrain.

"No, thank you. I'm stuffed," she replied honestly, patting her stomach.

She was sure that this piece of deliciousness had become her favorite sandwich. It was baked, and the melted cheese coating all the other ingredients was divine. She contemplated bringing a dozen back home with her.

Or trying to steal an original recipe.

"Are you sure?" Mason asked in false concern. "You will need your stamina tonight." He was obviously teasing her.

"I'm sure. However, you should worry about your own stamina," she replied in the same manner, barely keeping a straight face.

"Oh, you tease." He quickly kissed her on the mouth before going away to pay for their snack.

Afterward, they continued exploring. They visited the city park, Museum of Art, and St. Louis Cathedral. She took a lot of pictures so she could show them to her mom.

The days flew by without a single argument. Everything felt so easy for them in New Orleans that Ashlyn had half a mind to suggest they move there. If anything, being in New Orleans got her away from that eerie feeling of being followed back home. Here she was completely free and hadn't experienced even an ounce of fear or anxiety. That alone was reason enough to want to move there.

That was silly, of course. Their lives were back in Tahoe, her whole family, and she could never leave them, although it was a nice fantasy for a moment.

Ashlyn felt her hope that they would stay together and grow old together rekindle.

She experienced only one moment of doubt, and it was on their way home. As Mason drove them back, Ashlyn started to worry if all of this would last once they returned to their everyday lives.

As though he could read her mind, Mason presented her with a small box.

"What's this?"

"Open it and find out," he replied with a cryptic smile.

Inside was a beautiful diamond ring.

"What is this for?" she asked, instantly putting it on. It fit her perfectly, not that she'd doubted it would. Mason was meticulous like that.

"Something to remember our trip by," he replied.

It was obvious that while she wasn't looking, he'd sneaked to a jewelry store to surprise her. Her heart warmed.

He loved her that much, which was reassuring since she loved him beyond any measure as well.

"I would kiss you, but I don't want us to crash," she said, overcome with emotion.

Mason chuckled. "You can do whatever you like once we get home."

She intended to.

"I love it. I will never take it off," she said, looking at her new piece of jewelry.

"Promise?"

"I promise."

12

Ashlyn couldn't stop smiling as Mason drove them home. The time away had allowed them to reconnect, and it felt as though they'd hit a reset button. This was how it had been between them at the beginning of their relationship, and she was grateful it wasn't lost. It was still there within them. They just needed a reminder.

Before the trip, Ashlyn had been full of negativity, but she felt completely different now. It was as though a piece of her heart returned to her, the part that was missing, and she was fully at peace again. She felt liberated and full of positive thoughts, emotions, and energy. Just the way it was supposed to be.

She couldn't wait to be home, the same home she'd started to hate in a way. Although hate was probably the wrong word. She'd started to associate it with negative emotions, but that was a thing of the past. She was excited to return now that all the bad was firmly behind them.

It was a three-day drive, and Mason insisted that they push through without unnecessary breaks. Although the drive was tedious, Ashlyn still preferred it over flying. She had an all-consuming fear of flying, and luckily, her husband had consideration for her phobia. Besides, part of her thought he preferred driving. He liked being behind the wheel and in control.

They stopped at a hotel to sleep and continued first thing the next morning. The sun was setting as they approached their home.

"I have back-to-back meetings tomorrow, so I can't promise when I'll return home," he said somewhat apologetically.

Back to reality, she thought with somewhat mixed feelings. "That's fine. I'll be busy, too," she said.

"I'm too tired to park in the garage," Mason confessed.

"I don't care where you park. Let's just get inside." She couldn't wait to shower, go to bed, and sleep late. She needed to rest. She needed a mini vacation from her amazing vacation, she joked to herself.

"Agreed." Mason put the key in the lock and opened the door. "That's strange. The alarm didn't go off."

Entering the house, Ashlyn gasped. It took her a moment to truly process what she was seeing. "Oh, my God!"

Mason dropped all the bags, making her jump.

The interior of their once beautiful home was completely trashed. Even from the hall, she could see that the living room furniture was shredded as though with scissors or a sharp knife, all the carefully chosen pieces of art were destroyed, and tables were overturned and broken.

It looked as though a tornado had passed through it. But it was no act of God, it was the deed of a human being, because evidence of someone drinking and eating was everywhere. This was obviously a break-in.

As though spellbound, Ashlyn wanted to go inside and see if anything was salvageable. Who would do this to her lovely home? She'd worked so hard to create the perfect space, and now it was all gone like it never existed.

Mason stopped her, grabbing her hands. "Ashlyn, get in the car and call 911," he commanded.

She just looked at him. Why would she do that?

Her husband had to grab and shake her since she'd obviously slipped into shock without realizing it. "Whoever did this could still be in the house," he rushed to explain. "Go now," he practically growled.

He'd never spoken to her like that before, but it did the trick. Ashlyn ran outside and jumped inside the car, locking all the doors, too late realizing she had no idea where her phone was.

She started to panic, looking around, as though it would magically appear in front of her.

She was worried sick about Mason. He was unarmed inside, and if he was right, he was not alone. And this person who trashed their house had proven to be deranged.

What should I do? Her mind started to spin. They had a landline, so should she return to the house? Mason wouldn't like that. She knew that much.

Only then did she realize she was clutching her purse. She was definitely in shock.

The phone's inside, you idiot, she scoffed at herself, reaching for her cell.

Dialing the police, she held her breath, waiting for it to pass through. *Why is this taking so long?*

When she heard a pleasant-sounding voice asking what her emergency was, relief washed over her.

Ashlyn tried her best to explain what happened to them.

She was not sure how successful she was. "Please hurry. My husband is inside."

"Where are you?" the operator asked.

"Outside, in the car."

"Can you see what's happening inside?"

"No, I can't. Please hurry. There's a chance whoever did this is still inside."

"Is someone hurt?"

She started to say no, then reconsidered. "I don't know."

"Help is on the way. Remain where you are until the officers arrive," she advised.

Ashlyn nodded although the other woman couldn't see her.

As she disconnected, she heard a loud crash coming from inside the house, and that made her jump. Mason had left all the lights off, so she had no idea what was happening.

Oh, my God. The realization finally came to mind. Mason had been right. The burglar was still inside the house. And Mason was obviously fighting him. Ashlyn was horrified.

Another crash echoed through the silence.

Oh, my God, oh, my God, please don't let him die. Don't let my husband die.

As she prayed, like her mother had taught her so many years ago, there was a loud bang like a gunshot.

Ashlyn screamed. "Mason!" she cried out, half-deranged, in tears, rushing out of the car.

13

Ashlyn watched in horror as Mason stumbled out of the house and passed out. He was covered in blood and clutching his arm. He was bleeding to death, dying right in front of her eyes, and there was nothing she could do.

Luckily, the police came with the ambulance right behind them, and the paramedics rushed to help him.

In haste, she tried to explain what happened as the police started searching the grounds for the person who'd hurt Mason.

He was too badly injured to be helped on site, so he was put on a gurney. As the paramedics started to wheel him away, Mason revived just long enough to protest. He didn't want to leave, but nobody paid him any mind.

Ashlyn rode in the ambulance with him, but she couldn't even hold his hands and tell him she was there with him because the paramedic worked over him, clearly trying to save his life. The ride to the hospital took forever, and her mom's words came to her when she insisted that Ashlyn should not live that far from civilization.

What if something happens? Back then, she'd found that statement ridiculous, but now she saw how foolish and ignorant she had been.

Ashlyn paced in the waiting room while the doctors took care of her husband. Every once in a while, a nurse would come in to check up on her and share updates, clearly taking pity on her miserable appearance.

Somehow, she felt like this was all her fault. If they'd stayed home, then there would have been no break-in, and Mason would be just fine.

The diagnosis was that he'd lost a lot of blood due to a deep gash on his forearm where apparently the intruder had slashed at him with a knife. He bled excessively thanks to the adrenaline rush, which was also the reason he didn't know he was in such bad shape in the first place.

As she waited for the doctors to patch Mason up, someone from the police department came to speak with her. He introduced himself as Deputy Nelson.

Unfortunately, they hadn't found anyone around the vicinity of the house, he started by saying, which was very bad news if you asked her. She wanted this person caught and punished for what they'd done to Mason.

And then he asked her to tell him what happened.

"We were in New Orleans for the last week, and when we returned, we found the house completely trashed."

"Was someone inside?"

"Mason believed so, and he went in while I went outside to call the police."

"What happened next?"

"I don't know. I never went inside, but I heard noises of a

struggle and then a gunshot." She started to get upset all over again. "And the next thing I knew, Mason came out, covered in blood, holding his arm."

Ashlyn was still pretty shocked by the fact that Mason apparently owned a gun and had failed to tell her. She didn't like that. She thought there were no secrets between them.

Although part of her was glad he had been able to defend himself, the rest didn't know how she felt about it. It was a dangerous weapon, a thing that was deadly in the right and wrong hands. She wasn't completely comfortable with something like that within her walls.

Maybe that's why he didn't tell me in the first place.

All the same, if Mason hadn't had that weapon at his disposal, they could have both ended up dead. Mason had saved their lives, so she was ready to give him some slack for not telling her.

"We found some blood inside the house, but not the assailant."

"Maybe they escaped through a window or door in the back. I didn't see anyone come out of the front," Ashlyn provided. "I'm so sorry I don't know anything else," she added somewhat apologetically.

"That's all right, Mrs. Adams. I will take a statement from your husband when he's well enough."

"Of course."

"One more thing. When the forensics team is done, you will be able to return to your house. I will call you," he said.

"Thank you."

And then she waited. Ashlyn was all alone in the waiting room with her worried thoughts. She knew Mason would be all right. He had to be.

And then she realized she'd failed to call her family to let them know what happened.

Should I call his parents? she fleetingly thought before dismissing it. Mason wouldn't like that.

And she thought it best not to call her own family, either. Before doing anything, she wanted to know how her husband was. Besides, it was the middle of the night. No point in alarming them for something no longer life-threatening.

Finally, a nurse came to tell her he was all patched up and wheeled to his room as they spoke. So, she went to speak with his doctor before visiting him.

He'd received a partial transfusion and needed stitches in his arm. The surgery went a little longer than expected because some more sensitive parts got damaged. It was all very technical, yet she understood the gist.

"Will he be all right?"

"With some physical therapy, he will recover all motor function of the arm," the doctor reassured her.

She was relieved.

"He received a round of antibiotics, which is standard procedure, and some painkillers that'll make him feel a bit loopy for a bit."

"Thank you very much, Doctor."

"When he wakes up, he's fit to leave," he added.

Ashlyn found that surprising but didn't question it.

It was close to morning when Ashlyn signed the discharge papers. Mason looked drugged up and semi-coherent as she helped him get into a taxi.

"How are you feeling, Mason?" she asked for like the hundredth time in the last five minutes.

"Strange," he said, then proceeded to smack his lips together as though his lips felt funny or something.

Ashlyn was beyond concerned. Her husband rarely even drank a glass of wine, so taking heavy-duty painkillers messed him up. He constantly dozed off, and she let him.

They had a bit of a ride ahead of them, so if he could sleep it off, that would be for the better. At least those were her thoughts.

When they arrived at their house, she paid for the ride and thanked the taxi driver, who even helped with getting her husband out of the car. Very slowly, the two of them managed to reach the front door.

Being confronted with the horror that transpired triggered her, and her eyes swelled with tears again. She'd almost lost him.

Ashlyn stopped herself, knowing she needed to be strong now. Not because Mason needed her emotional support but because he needed her quite literally. If she couldn't see where they were going because of the tears, then they were both doomed, since he was still pretty drugged up.

"Look at this," he muttered in horror, looking around.

"Never mind that, Mason. Let's get you to bed," she rushed to say, carefully moving him forward.

"Your home. Your beautiful home," he said with remorse. "I can't believe that asshole did this."

"We're both safe and alive. That's all that matters."

Thankfully, he allowed himself to be steered toward the bedrooms. Getting up the stairs was a challenge, but they managed.

She wanted to kick herself for not allowing him to stay downstairs, but then again, where would he sleep? The couch was completely trashed.

And besides, there was no way she would leave him there, in all that filth, garbage, and broken furniture.

Ignoring the remnants of her life, she put Mason to bed. She was horrified to see blood in their master bedroom, so she put him in one of the guest rooms to sleep off the medication.

As she tucked him in, he started to mutter quite angrily. Was his arm bothering him? It wasn't supposed to, considering he was on painkillers.

"What did you say, Mason?" she asked softly.

Perhaps he needed something to drink.

"That asshole tried to ruin everything."

Ashlyn frowned. *Who is he talking about? The intruder? Or one of the clients he doesn't like?*

"Stupid idiot," he added before starting to snore quite soundly.

He was clearly delusional, dreaming about nonsense while awake. Those were some strong meds. She wished she had some so she could face their trashed home.

Knowing full well that there would be no sleeping for her, although she had just spent the entire night in the hospital, she returned downstairs.

She had to walk around a huge bloodstain to get to the sink and get a glass of water. Taking it all in, she reconsidered. She couldn't deal with all of it tonight. She didn't want to disturb Mason, so she went to a different guest room, lay down fully clothed, and fell asleep almost instantly.

All too soon, her phone awoke her. It was an unknown number, but she answered, nevertheless.

"Good morning, Mrs. Adams." She was still groggy but recognized the voice.

"Good morning, Deputy. What can I do for you?" she

asked politely, checking what time it was. It was barely eight, which meant she'd slept three whole hours. *Yay.*

"I just wanted to let you know that the forensics team did their job. They took pictures and collected samples, so you're welcome to return home."

Of course, she'd completely forgotten they were supposed to wait. Luckily, she hadn't messed anything up.

"Shoot, we returned last night," she fretted. "I hope that's not a problem."

"No, that's fine. We finished early in the evening, but thought you'd be at the hospital until later today. I should have called sooner."

"Oh, well, all right. Thank you for calling now."

"Hey, just one more thing."

"Yes."

"The forensic unit will need a sample of your husband's blood."

"Why?"

"Well, they collected samples from the house and want to rule him out."

"Do you think some of it could be the intruder's?"

"That's the idea."

So there was a possibility that this lunatic could be found based on DNA, as she saw in the movies? That was great news.

"Mason is still asleep, and the doctor forbade him any physical activity for a few days."

"That's all right. Come down to the sheriff's office whenever you can," he was quick to reassure.

"Will do."

After she disconnected, she went to check on Mason. He was still down for the count. She made sure he was comfortable enough and not pressuring his wound in any way, and then she changed clothes and went downstairs.

She felt like weeping. She was stunned, not knowing where to start cleaning.

Her mom would tell her to pick one task and start from there, so that was exactly what she did. Taking some trash bags, she started throwing away all she could. As she went, she inspected a few furniture pieces and was cheered to discover the coffee table could be fixed.

The sofa cushions were completely gutted, so she threw away what she could and left the rest, realizing she would need professional help to get rid of the bigger pieces. Her heart broke for all the custom things she had to get rid of, but they were beyond repair.

She tried to tell herself that it was only stuff, that she should not feel so attached, but it didn't help. She'd invested a lot of her time and energy into creating this space, and someone had come and completely destroyed it. That was not fair.

Then again, life was like that.

Filling the last of the bags and carrying it outside, she moved on to the next task. Getting rid of all the bloodstains. She couldn't look at them, so she Googled the best ways to deal with them and then went to work.

She worked hard and without breaks, wanting the house to be completely blood-free before Mason woke. She didn't want him to encounter all of that upon waking. He had been through enough and deserved a chance to heal in peace.

Needing to fill in the silence with something, she listened to the news on her laptop since the TV was broken.

"The search for nineteen-year-old Amanda Lacey is still active. And her parents ask you to contact them or the police if you see her," she heard the speaker say as she scrubbed the floor.

She looked over at the screen and was startled to see that the woman looked very similar to her, although younger.

Wasn't she the second redhead to go missing? How many were there now? Three? Four? She couldn't quite remember.

Ashlyn felt a shiver of fear slide down her back. *Who the hell was taking these women and what were they doing with them?*

14

The next couple of days were pretty hectic. Mason was grumpy at having to stay home and do nothing, so he played a lot of video games since he said it helped with his injured arm.

Ashlyn was happy he was staying out of her hair, because having him around in that peculiar mood was not helping with hers, especially since she had a ton of things to do.

It took her almost a whole week to deal with the insurance company, and it would have lasted longer if Mason hadn't stepped in and started threatening. With that done, she could concentrate on rebuilding her broken home.

She took out everything that the intruder had destroyed. Thankfully, Mason called a service and hired a temporary maid, Missy, so she didn't have to do everything on her own. It was a sweet gesture and Ashlyn was grateful for it. Still, even between the two of them, there was a lot to be done.

One door had to be replaced since it looked like someone had tried to hack it, which looked completely insane to her. If she didn't know better, she would think this was personal. But she guessed having a crazy person break inside was equally damaging.

Eventually, she told her family that a deranged man had broken in and fought with Mason, but she downplayed it, not wanting to concern them too much. Her mother offered to come help with the cleaning, but Ashlyn didn't want to trouble her.

"It's okay, Mom. Missy and I have it all covered," she said.

"Whatever you say, but please come to Sunday dinner. We miss you."

"Sure thing, Mom."

Ashlyn realized she liked being busy because that way, she didn't have time to think about what happened that night and what she could have lost.

Some man had broken into their home and destroyed everything. As though that was not enough, he'd attacked Mason. Watching him pass out in front of her eyes was one of the most frightening, painful things she'd ever experienced. So, she tried to avoid thinking because thinking put her back to that moment, which made her emotional, weepy, and overall, a mess.

She couldn't get over the fact that something like that had happened. Those kinds of things were not supposed to happen in real life, only in movies. And she was very much aware that she seemed ridiculous, considering that worse things than mere break-ins happened every day.

Ashlyn didn't feel safe anymore. She couldn't speak with Mason about it because he was healing, and she didn't want to burden him. Besides, she knew what his response would be. They were protected. They had an alarm system and all the other crap. And yes, she'd intentionally used the word "crap" because they'd had all of that before the break-in as well, and it had done nothing to prevent it.

Maybe we should get a dog, she mused.

Ashlyn knew she had to do something, because living in fear was exhausting. She became so jumpy that even Mason noticed something was up.

She wanted that man caught. Only then would she be able to sleep peacefully at night. It didn't help that the police had no clue how someone broke into their home in the first place. They would normally suspect it was a professional job, but nothing had been taken. Everything had been destroyed.

Was it some new form of eco-terrorism? She grasped at straws. Or was this man just insane? Regardless of the motives, one question remained the same. How did he break in?

Mason and Ashlyn lived in the middle of nowhere and had a state-of-the-art security system—*what a joke*—yet this man had still managed to get inside and trash everything.

How? Why?

If he wanted to rob them, then why hadn't he? Why did he linger and have a rage fest, destroying everything?

Did the person know she and Mason would be away? That was highly unlikely. Unless... what if it was the person who had been following her around Tahoe? What if they'd come here to hurt her and found her gone then got mad and trashed the place? The idea of that made Ashlyn even more paranoid, but Mason wouldn't even listen to her attempt to explain her fear. He just told her not to worry, that he'd protect her.

The police theorized that the intruder was squatting and

was likely mentally unstable since he'd stabbed Mason before jumping through a window.

In a way, that theory fit. It was as good as any, she supposed, better than her own at any rate, until they caught him and asked him what on earth he was doing.

To be perfectly honest, Mason was handling all this much better than she was. She'd become nervous, distracted, paranoid, and distraught, so at times, he had to comfort her even though it should have been the other way around because he was the injured one. All the same, she couldn't stop feeling the way she did.

Part of her wished they could move. Of course, she kept that to herself. She could never ask her husband to do something like that. Not after all the effort, time, and love he'd invested into creating this space for them.

So she focused on keeping herself busy, repairing all the damage, and trying to move on with her life.

The police had no real evidence against the man who broke inside, only some partial prints that led them nowhere, blood that didn't pop up in their database and the fact that whoever this man was, he'd been able to get past their state-of-the-art alarm system, so Mason agreed to go to the sheriff's department and sit with a sketch artist to describe the attacker.

Ashlyn went with him just in case he needed her, and also because she didn't feel like staying home alone. She told Mason it was because she liked driving him around.

He rolled his eyes because he thought that was a man's job.

They didn't stay long. Mason gave clear instructions to the sketch artist. The other man was impressed, but Ashlyn knew he was great with details. She considered that an occupational hazard. While the two of them worked, she chatted with Deputy Nelson. He didn't have any news to share and was hopeful this sketch would be helpful in identifying the burglar.

Part of her felt guilty that they were wasting their time with this case when there were those women missing. Then again, she was sure there were other people on those cases as well.

"So this is the man who attacked you?" the artist asked, holding up the image he'd drawn.

Mason looked at it and nodded. "Yes, that's him." He was very matter-of-fact, almost nonchalant.

Ashlyn barely glanced at the sketch—all she caught was a scruffy beard, and messy hair—she didn't want to see the guy's face because she was afraid it would give her nightmares. She turned away, and looked toward the door.

Mason joined her and took her hand, drawing her up to stand.

"Good luck catching him," Mason offered as they started toward the door, but then he stopped and looked back at the sheriff. "And just so you know, if I catch him first, you'll be dealing with a dead man."

"Sir—" the sheriff started.

Mason gave him a cold look. "I will protect what is mine."

The sheriff gave him a nod after a moment. "Thank you for coming."

He didn't sound as happy and grateful as he had a few minutes earlier, and she couldn't blame him at all for that. Mason had sounded a little scary. Almost like he was threatening them that he'd find this guy and do their job for them.

A shiver of fear slid down her spine as they stepped out of the police station.

The car ride back was silent. It was on the tip of her tongue to suggest they should stop and visit her parents, but she didn't. She was afraid of pissing him off more, but then he didn't really seem angry. Maybe she'd misunderstood what he'd meant? Maybe he'd been in such pain it had caused him to sound more harsh than he'd meant. That had to be it. He was probably just in pain. Besides, she was sure Mason needed some rest after dealing with all of this.

She hoped they would catch this man because she feared he might return. No matter how irrational that sounded, that was the fear she lived with every day. That was what kept her wide awake at night, especially when Mason wasn't by her side.

15

Ashlyn considered what to do about all the rooms that had been damaged in the break-in.

Mason advised her to contact her suppliers and buy all the same things, custom-make everything she couldn't, and be done with it. His heart was in the right place. He didn't want her to stress about it because the more she worked on it, the longer it would take her to forget what happened and move on.

She thought about it, but eventually ruled against it. It wouldn't matter if she bought all the same things. She would know that they were replicas, and that would torment her and remind her of what happened, and she definitely didn't want that.

So, she took a different approach. She would redo everything and think of it as remodeling. Granted, it came much sooner than she expected, or wanted it to, *but hey, that's life.* Besides, this way she would have two houses to showcase her business. That was certainly a bright side in a world of darkness.

Mason disagreed at first. However, after reassuring him that this would be more therapeutic for her, he agreed to it.

With that settled, she started to brainstorm, designing everything from scratch. This time around, she would do it in a different style and choose different colors because after being vandalized, they deserved a fresh start and a space that suggested just that.

Ashlyn dug out all her old notebooks with notes about room dimensions and scratched ideas to make sure she remembered them right.

If she were that senile, she would be worried, she joked.

Since this time around, she was actually in the house and not forced to rely on Mason, she did some measurements on her own and afterward was quite confused by some things.

She noticed that some of the rooms were smaller on the inside than they should be. And some walls were unnecessarily thick. *Why did Mason do that?* She would understand if those were outside walls that protected them from the elements, but it made no sense to have such walls on the inside.

Was it soundproofed? All kinds of thoughts passed through her head. *I must be doing something wrong,* she mused, looking at her notes, completely baffled.

Seeing no other way, she decided to ask Mason if she could see the original blueprints since these dimensions made no sense to her.

He had been working from his office for the last couple of days. Technically, he was still on home rest, but that didn't stop him from conducting business as well.

Ashlyn let him be. She knew that sitting around the

house and doing nothing must be pure torture for him. He was a workaholic, after all.

As she entered his office, she found him sitting behind his desk, as always. He was on the phone and furiously typing on his computer. Mason did not look pleased with whomever he was speaking to.

His home office was the first room they'd worked on. The damage here hadn't been significant. They'd thoroughly cleaned it and replaced a few broken things.

Mason ordered the same things he had before they were destroyed, and they were delivered a day later. And now it looked just the way he wanted it, as though nothing bad had ever happened.

Someday soon, the rest of the house would look like that as well.

"I understand that," Mason's deep, unyielding voice snapped her from her reverie. "However, if you want to complain about delays, you certainly don't come knocking on my door."

He paused there, as though listening. His frown was so deep, she could see it across the room.

"Look, you have all the blueprints, which means at this stage, my work is done." Mason was adamant. "I don't care about that," he added after a small break, his voice firm, but he sounded stressed.

Ashlyn hated seeing him like this. He was still recovering and already under a lot of stress. That couldn't be good for him.

There was some continuous back and forth between Mason and his caller, during which Ashlyn seriously considered just leaving him be. He was obviously in the middle of some serious work, and she didn't want to impose.

She made a move to leave the office when he motioned her with his good arm to stay, so she did.

She sat in one of the leather chairs across from his desk and waited patiently.

After several more minutes of arguing, the conversation ended. Ashlyn couldn't be one hundred percent sure, but she believed her husband came out of it the victor.

Of course he did, she thought proudly.

She stood up to give him a kiss before returning to her seat.

"What is it, my love?" he asked.

"Problems?" she inquired.

He looked at her oddly. "What do you mean?"

"The phone call sounded heated."

He waved with his hand, then winced, obviously realizing too late that he had used the wrong one. "Usual bullshit. This asshole of a client doesn't understand how business is conducted."

"Is he important?"

Mason made a face. "In a way. A movie star." He started to massage his injured arm.

Ashlyn was sure that was an unconscious act. He did that a great deal when stressed, she noted. That troubled her.

"I'm sure you can handle one movie star," she tried to lighten the mood.

"Of course I can," he replied with a grin. "So, did you need anything?" he added, grabbing his mobile phone.

Although she had his attention, it was obvious he was busy, but he had asked and she knew he cared about the designs as much as she did, so she said, "Well, I was going over the measurements for the house, and I had a question."

"Okay, what is it?"

"I know you're the architect and you know all this stuff, but I was curious as to why some of the walls seem thicker than others."

He shook his head. "Oh, that. Well, some of them are load-bearing walls and needed thickness for support, others, like our bedroom, I soundproofed. You know I can't sleep when I hear any kind of noise."

His reply made total sense and Ashlyn smiled. "I knew you would have an answer." She hopped up from her chair. "I also wanted to see if you'd like something to eat. I'm making sandwiches." She did want to try and recreate those delicious sandwiches from New Orleans.

"That would be great, thank you."

"No problem," she replied with a smile.

"I'll be in here about half an hour more, and then we can eat together."

"Perfect."

"Come and give me a kiss before you go."

That made her smile. Despite all the seriousness, her husband was also silly, if only with her. That was why she happily went to him to get her kiss before carrying on with her day.

16

All the repairs and remodeling were finished, and life slowly returned to normal.

The relationship between Ashlyn and Mason was far better than it had been before the trip to New Orleans. He'd been very attentive toward her while they were there, fulfilling her every dream, every fantasy, and once they'd returned, he'd defended her with his life, which showed he truly loved her.

However, she still had a gnawing doubt inside.

She couldn't fully decide if things were calm because they'd reached some kind of a breakthrough during that trip or because she had been very careful around him.

At first, she was tentative because he was injured and didn't want to upset him while he was healing, yet because she still feared that he was cheating on her, she continued to walk on eggshells. She was afraid to ruffle any feathers as she watched for signs that he was returning to his previous behavior, because that would be definite proof that the trip had been all for nothing, that they were seriously broken without repair.

Naturally, there was a chance this was all in her head and nothing would change dramatically even if they had a fight every once in a while, like any other normal couple.

To be perfectly fair, there was a possibility that Mason was doing the same with her. Walking on eggshells so as not to rock the boat. He was home with her more, working from his office there, and just attentive enough she couldn't complain. He'd ordered enough food and drinks for the house to last weeks, as though stocking a bunker for Armageddon. However, Ashlyn wondered if he was doing it because he wanted to avoid any kind of possible confrontation. This way he could say, *See? I'm involved. I take care of you and your needs.*

It all felt kind of calculating from both sides, and that confounded her. Why were they doing this? Were they both afraid of failure, or of the other person leaving? The not knowing was driving her crazy. Ashlyn felt like she needed professional help to sort through the mess in her head, yet how to make Mason see that was what their marriage needed?

Everything looked perfect on the surface. She had a caring husband. She was a devoted wife. But at times, she felt like Mason kept a big chunk of himself hidden away from her.

What is he hiding? She quickly dismissed the thought. She was exaggerating like she normally did. The problem was that her business wasn't going as well as it should, and now she had nothing better to do than sit around in her office all day and wait for her husband to come home.

Which was something she'd vowed she would never do. And while she waited, she analyzed each and every interaction between them. No wonder she was going mad. Any sane person would be.

She wished she was confident enough to think only about the good things, but she wasn't. And all this stress wasn't helping her or her marriage. Especially when things between them were good.

Was she intentionally trying to sabotage a good thing to justify her feelings? That made her pause. It was possible. Because Mason was trying to make her happy. He'd even suggested date nights about two weeks ago.

Once a week, they went out all dressed up, and that was just one more example of how Mason put in an effort to please her. The devil in her still felt like that wasn't enough. They spent one night out together, and what about the other six? During those, he was more content to eat dinner and then go back to work in his office or play video games in his man cave than to be with her, and it was hard not to feel resentful.

Ashlyn wanted more from her marriage and more from her husband. And in the midst of all that insanity, she felt guilty for feeling like that. She didn't want to appear greedy because she was very grateful for her life.

It wasn't like she didn't know Mason's work was a priority when they got together. Right from the start, she'd had to accept his long hours at the office, business dinners, and trips.

When he returned to working at his office in Tahoe full-time—once his arm had fully healed—Mason started staying late at the office, missing dinner with her and coming home at such late hours she was usually asleep long before then.

They started spending less and less time together. When he was actually at home, he was either in his office finishing work or in the basement playing video games, which didn't leave much time for the two of them for romance and intimacy. Or even for more mundane things that went with sharing a life with another person.

Is he cheating? Ashlyn wondered. It was hard not to roll her eyes at herself. She sounded like a character from a novel, where a woman suspects her husband is cheating. Still... there was something off about him.

He claimed he had to work late because he was going to physical therapy for part of the day while at work. And she couldn't resent that he was seeing his doctor and wanting to get better, although she missed him greatly. They spent so little time together, she constantly felt like a thirsty man in a desert who was allowed only a few drops of water each morning.

Was she exaggerating? Probably. But that was how she felt.

Mason had received that wound defending her and their home, so of course, he had to do everything in his power to return to the best health possible. She wanted that for him, especially since he needed both hands to draw his future projects.

She felt so alone, abandoned. Since she was her mother's daughter, that also made her feel guilty as hell. Here she was, complaining about her woes, when she had everything —a comfortable life, and a loving husband.

The problem had to be her, not him, because Mason was trying.

Still, Ashlyn felt stuck between what her head said and what her heart felt, and the sad part was she didn't know how to change that. Maybe she needed to go to therapy on her own?

17

"Please don't kill me," Ashlyn pleaded as tears streamed down her face. She was cornered, pressed against the bedroom window, as the attacker advanced. "No, please don't."

In return, her stalker screamed like a monster from hell, a lunatic escaped from the asylum, a thing from nightmares.

Ashlyn had no idea how this deranged man had entered her home, yet ever since she'd opened her eyes, she was trying to escape him and his huge knife, running through the house, calling out for help. She realized she was alone inside the house with that maniac. They were alone in the middle of nowhere.

Ashlyn tried her best to escape. The floor was very slippery for some reason, and she slipped a lot, injuring her left ankle.

You have to escape, she tried to encourage herself.

The monster practically salivated while looking at her, switching the blade between hands.

He's going to kill me. The fear was almost paralyzing, but something deep inside her—call it a survival instinct—refused to let her give up.

Ashlyn dashed from her corner, avoiding being stabbed by an inch, and ran with all her might toward the front door.

The house looked bigger, way bigger than it was supposed to, and no matter how much she tried, she could not find the end of the hallway and the steps that led to the ground floor.

What is happening here? *Was she drugged?*

She knew he was right behind her, wanting to murder her.

What was the point? There's no escaping this place, *she thought in exasperation, slowing down.*

Don't you dare give up, *she screamed at herself.*

Ashlyn needed to escape, to alert everyone about what was happening here. She'd found the killer. He was inside this house.

She dared to turn around to see where her stalker was, and regretted it instantly. A faceless man, who laughed the whole time as he ran, was gaining on her and slashing the air with the blade. Ashlyn tripped, and the knife barely missed her face.

They screamed at the same time. Deciding to hide in one of the rooms, Ashlyn dashed inside and found herself in the kitchen. She almost felt relief getting to the back door.

Ashlyn screamed as she pulled on the handle and the thing would not budge.

No, no, no. *The door was locked.*

Where is the key? *she asked herself as she frantically looked about. She had no idea. She was going to die there because there was no escaping this damned house.*

"Please, can somebody help me?" *she screamed with all her might, banging against the glass door. She could see only darkness on the outside.*

She was alone, trapped.

Ashlyn turned to face her attacker. There was nothing around her she could use to defend herself. She was trapped and weaponless. I will die now.

Her vision blurred from all the tears, and she had to strain to see anything. She had no idea why she bothered. She didn't want to see that maniac's hideous face before he stabbed her.

"Why are you doing this?" Ashlyn yelled at the approaching attacker. "What do you want from me?"

Without uttering a word, the killer raised the knife and in one swift move slashed downward.

Before the knife was plunged into her heart, Ashlyn opened her eyes and gasped for air. She was covered in sweat and crying inconsolably, shaking from the intensity of her emotions. She felt like she was about to die. And no amount of *it was only a dream, calm down, you're safe* helped in the slightest.

It felt so real that her brain had trouble readjusting. *They don't call them night terrors without reason.*

Ashlyn hated nightmares. Then again, she was sure there was not a person on this planet who loved them. They were nothing more than personal torture devices.

Why do people have them in the first place? She had no idea. It wasn't like she was unaware that she still struggled with what had happened. Not only had she been stalked—was still being stalked—while she was out and about in Tahoe, but a person had broken into their home, destroyed everything, and hurt Mason so badly that he was still going to physical therapy. Was it the same person? she wondered. Had they tracked her down? Ashlyn had no idea if her thoughts were rational or not and she had no idea how to overcome her fears. Since the attack, she had stopped feeling safe in her own home, and that was the worst feeling imaginable. Her mother had been right all along. Not that she would tell her that.

She really didn't need her crazy brain coming up with

these kinds of slasher-movie scenarios to torment her. She had enough worries as it was. Perhaps the problem was that she wasn't doing anything about it. Then again, what *could* she do? Move? That was not an option.

Make the house more secure? It was already a freaking fortress. There wasn't much more she could do apart from hiring twenty-four seven security. And she didn't want to live that way. There was no privacy in a house like that. Besides, it would make her feel like she was a drug dealer or something.

So, she had to endure and hope the bad dreams would go away in time. She hoped that would occur sooner rather than later because the lack of sleep was seriously messing with her head.

The most troubling part of those dreams wasn't the deranged maniac holding a knife and chasing her around the house. It was the fact that she was all alone. Mason was nowhere to be seen. More to the point, she hadn't even thought of looking for him, calling out for him.

That was the biggest telltale of all. It showed how she felt about her husband and their marriage. Even in the midst of the greatest danger, she couldn't turn to him and ask for his help because it seemed as though he was never there.

She was all alone in real life, so she was all alone in her nightmares as well.

It was just sad.

Not even now, upon waking from such a disturbing dream, in tears and completely rattled, could she rely on him. Because he was not there with her, although it was pretty late.

Did he fall asleep in his man cave again? she thought, slightly irked. It definitely wouldn't be the first time. He'd said that sometimes the video gaming helped him nod off, and while that was great, she didn't like the fact that he wasn't in bed next to her.

Wiping the tears away, she took a few deep breaths and tried to calm down. After a couple of minutes, nothing changed.

Feeling restless, she left the bed and went in search of her husband.

The house looked empty.

Just like in my dream. She banished that immediately. She didn't want to think about that at all. Still, the feeling of uneasiness persisted.

Ashlyn reached the basement door. "Mason?" she called out.

There was no reply. She tried the handle, but the door was locked. She frowned. That was weird.

After a very short debate with herself, she texted him.

> Where are you?

She waited and waited, but there was no reply. Was he asleep down there?

Five minutes later, Ashlyn went to the kitchen to drink some water, and afterward, she settled in a chair, tapping her phone against the kitchen counter as though that would change anything.

Where is that man? She decided she was not going to bed until she spoke with him. She decided to call him. It rang a couple of times before he picked up.

"Mmm, Ashlyn, sweetheart, what's wrong?" He sounded groggy.

"I woke up and you weren't in bed, and I came downstairs to look for you and you didn't answer when I knocked. I got worried," Ashlyn replied, unable to keep the upset from her voice.

"I'll be right up. Give me a second, and we'll talk."

A moment later, she heard the door opening. Without waiting for him, she rose and went to greet him.

She was slightly startled by his appearance. Mason was wearing only his pajama bottoms and looked tired. He had definitely been asleep.

"There you are."

"Of course," he said, still sounding slightly groggy. "I couldn't sleep, so I went to watch a movie."

He always made sure not to disturb her. Usually, that was very sweet of him—that he wanted to make sure she got some rest.

"I tried the door, and it was locked," she pointed out.

He frowned and looked at the door. "It jams sometimes. I'll fix that." Taking a deep breath, he added, "What did you need? Why are you up so late?"

"I had a bad dream and couldn't find you," she complained, remembering that awful dream. "This person was chasing me, and I thought I was going to die."

"I'm sorry, sweetheart, but you have nothing to worry about. Nothing will hurt you here. It was just a dream, probably because of the jerk who broke in, but I promise I will protect you."

She nodded. "I know it's silly to be so upset by a dream, but still, I feel much better seeing you," she explained, giving him a hug.

Mason held her and patted her on the back, then kissed her temple. "Go back to sleep, my love."

"Are you coming with me?" she asked, hopeful.

"If you don't mind, I want to go finish the show I started. I don't think I'm going to get back to sleep anytime soon."

Ashlyn was disappointed, but she understood, at least about the insomnia part. Now that he was up, he wouldn't be able to go back to sleep right away. The problem was, she did need to go back to sleep. She'd made enough of a fool of herself as it was, crying to her husband over a stupid dream. Mason was right. She shouldn't let a dream get to her. She was an adult, not a child. Maybe she needed to start acting like it.

"All right," she said, unable to keep the disappointment from her tone. It was on the tip of her tongue to ask if she could join him for the rest of the movie, but she held back. That was his space down there in the basement, and she didn't want to intrude.

Ashlyn turned off all the lights before returning to bed. Mason watched her from the hall with his hand on the doorknob to his man cave as she climbed the stairs. Her heart felt heavy as he gave her a smile. She heard the door open as she passed out of his view.

She sighed as she continued toward the bedroom. She missed her husband. She was starting to feel the distance between them, especially now, but then she brushed it off. She realized she was being too emotional, probably because of the nightmare, and was exaggerating.

He couldn't sleep and was watching a movie. *End of story.*

Despite all the craziness the nightmare brought, Ashlyn forced herself to calm down and stop thinking about anything. She eventually managed to fall asleep, but the dreams she had were still very troubled.

18

"Why are you watching that?" Mason asked as he entered the living room.

Ashlyn was sitting on the couch, covered with a light blanket, watching a crime show special about kidnappings covering the whole psychology behind kidnappers.

She had figured the way things had been going, Mason would arrive home and instantly go to his man cave. It was what he'd done every night for the past week. Apparently, he'd decided to grace her with his presence for once.

Ashlyn abandoned that thought because it was too mean. Mason worked a lot to provide her with this life. To keep her safe. He was allowed some alone time. She needed to not take that personally.

They all needed that from time to time.

Maybe the problem is that you have more alone time than you need. She dismissed that thought as well. Only then did she remember that she'd failed to answer his question.

"I want to be informed on things going on around us," she replied.

The show she was watching was a documentary about the young women around Tahoe who had gone missing over the past year. The first one to go missing had been nineteen-year-old Amanda Lacey, who, quite disturbingly, looked like Ashlyn, with natural red hair, green eyes, and extremely pale skin. They'd come out with the documentary because another redhead, Natalie, had gone missing.

In all there were four young women that the police knew about—Amanda, Charlene, Olga, and now Natalie, all who resembled Ashlyn and had been abducted in the Tahoe area. Although it would be crazy to assume that fact would get her kidnapped tomorrow, it would also be foolish to completely ignore it. And there was the fact that several times now, while she had been in Tahoe, she'd felt as though she was being stalked. Was it this kidnapper? Did whoever this kidnapper was have their eyes on Ashlyn? Were they the one to break into her and Mason's home? The idea freaked her out.

The whole situation rattled her on a personal level, and it was hard not to succumb to fear. Sometimes in her nightmares, instead of that maniac chasing her with a knife, there was a masked man chasing her around the house, rambling about her hair and how much he wanted to possess her. She couldn't say what made her feel worse.

Because of her nightmares, and the fact that several women, who all seemed to look similar to her, had been kidnapped, Ashlyn had started to watch the news religiously in hopes she would learn something new. That was when she'd seen the local station was showing a documentary this evening after the latest kidnapping. She knew almost everything about each of the first three women and their disappearances, but tonight she was learning about the latest victim. Each day she had watched, though, she had hoped there would be a break in the case and the young women would be found alive.

From everything she'd learned so far, no one had called any of their parents to ask for a ransom, so according to the reporters that meant they weren't taken for money. That was even worse, as far as Ashlyn was concerned. There were a lot of crazy, disturbed, evil people in this world, so being taken for money was a lesser evil than the alternatives in her mind.

There was still hope, though, that all would end well, considering none of their bodies had been discovered yet. Ashlyn felt that surely, if this was a serial killer, he would have killed them by now. That sounded horrible, but that was the world they lived in. Ashlyn hung on to that belief that this would all have a happy ending. Because without hope, they had nothing.

"Why would you want to watch something so depressing?" Mason grumbled, coming to sit next to her.

She was surprised by his words. "Women are going missing, Mason."

"That may be true, but I'm afraid these reporters are just scaring people without reason," he countered, waving toward the TV. "These people are vultures and will use anything to get better ratings."

Ashlyn had to agree, if somewhat grudgingly, because that made sense, but only partially. "Four women—all redheads like me, mind you—have gone missing, and in this area. You cannot tell me that's not alarming," she insisted.

Mason scoffed a little, but then, after looking at her face, he relented. "No, something is clearly going on," he replied, nodding. "However, you have nothing to worry about. You're nothing like those women."

Ashlyn's brow furrowed. "What do you mean? They all look eerily similar to me, and I know I haven't said anything before, but... well... for the past several months, almost every time I go into Tahoe, I feel like I'm being stalked." Her words came out almost as a whisper.

"Ashlyn, seriously. This is no cause for alarm. You're probably just imagining things because these reporters are putting ideas in your head."

That didn't sit well with Ashlyn. "This kidnapper is taking redheads from our area, Mason, and I'm a redhead, and I just told you I feel like I'm being stalked," she repeated, feeling silly that she needed to point at herself while saying that. "What if whoever broke into our house was this kidnapper looking to come after me?"

Without saying anything in return, Mason opened his arms, and she went willingly. It always felt good in his arms. That was where she felt most cherished and protected.

"This serial kidnapper, or whatever you want to call him, won't harm you," he said in a soft voice. "I won't allow it. Didn't I run off the person who broke in?"

"I guess you're right. You did and got hurt in the process. But I still don't plan on leaving this house, ever," she countered, only partially joking.

Mason chuckled, holding her tighter. "You won't hear any argument from me."

She looked up at him.

"I like having you all to myself," he added as he kissed her temple.

Ashlyn sighed. "Joking aside, I'm truly worried." Especially since she was not the only redhead in her family. Her father and her younger sister shared the same traits. Not that she was worried about her dad.

"You're safe here, I promise. Crime is one of the reasons I wanted to move out of the city, remember?" he insisted.

Despite what she said seconds ago, she knew she couldn't stay hidden inside her house indefinitely because she was afraid. That wouldn't be rational. She needed to live her life, and it infuriated her that this kidnapper was threatening that.

"Those poor women," she said, burrowing her head in the crook of his neck and breathing his scent in, drawing comfort from it.

"I know. All the same, I have to say he has great taste in women," Mason said and laughed.

"That's not funny."

"I'm not joking. Look at them. They are beautiful women. Like you."

Ashlyn made a face, breaking the embrace immediately. Although she understood he was only trying to lighten the mood, this was taking things too far. It was definitely not funny. Those poor women who were kidnapped could not be a joking matter. "You're being gross," she warned.

"What?" he asked, looking confused.

"You cannot joke about such serious matters. Someone just lost a daughter, a sister, a loved one, and you're making light of it."

Mason sighed. "I was just pointing out the obvious. They are all beautiful women."

It was hard to not lash out at her husband. "I'm genuinely concerned about this, and you're making it worse," she tried to explain.

Mason frowned. He obviously didn't understand her anxiety over these kidnappings. "If you're so concerned, then maybe don't go into Tahoe. He can't kidnap you if you don't engage in risky behavior."

She couldn't decipher whether he was still joking or serious. Still, she said, "Risky behavior? What kind of behavior are you talking about?"

He nodded. "You know. Being out in the open, in the middle of the night, like easy prey," he said with a small shrug.

Ashlyn could only stare at her husband for a few heartbeats. Once she recovered from the initial shock, she said, "You're completely missing the point."

"Am I?" He again seemed confused.

"Yes."

"Then enlighten me."

"Someone is kidnapping women."

He stared at her as though she had two heads. "I know that, but what's that have to do with me? What do you want me to say?"

"I want you to show more empathy, not joke around and make me feel like I'm behaving irrationally."

He sighed again, clearly frustrated. "You *are* acting irrationally, though, sweetheart. Nobody is going to come after you, even if you are more beautiful than those women. I won't allow it to happen," he pointed out, which infuriated her even more.

In her mind, he was being obtuse, and it was making her angry. "You know what? Let's end this conversation. We clearly don't see eye to eye."

He shrugged, and ran a hand through his hair, sighing once again. "Already forgotten, my love. I'm going to go do some gaming," he said. And with that, he kissed her cheek, stood up, and headed for his man cave.

Ashlyn was so angry that she felt like throwing something at him, which was a level of fury she was not used to. It scared her that she had such high emotions over their argument. She had no idea how it even started. Was it even an argument?

His behavior was strange to her. It was as though he really couldn't see why she was so upset about women who looked like her going missing, and that infuriated her. And then it was like he just dismissed her feelings and went on about his day like nothing had happened. Like she wasn't very obviously upset. Ever since they'd moved here where he had his personal space to escape to, he'd started to ignore her feelings more and more often.

She missed the good old days when after a fight they would glare at one another across the dining room table until one of them caved and apologized. Come to think of it, they'd never fought like this, not while living in that old apartment.

She dismissed that because she was reaching. Their fights had nothing to do with their location and everything to do with them. Something had changed, and it showed.

Mason was definitely making things worse with these disappearing acts of his. They never managed to resolve anything because when he felt like he'd had enough, he walked away and left her reeling. That was not how communication worked. That was not how relationships worked. At least, not the good ones.

Was it too much to ask for a little comfort, a speck of understanding since this was something that actually bothered her? Apparently, it was. Her husband could be so oblivious at times.

He would rather crack insensitive, highly inappropriate jokes and advise her to stay home and never leave like a good little wife should than actually be there for her. And then, on top of everything else, he just disappeared on her.

Ashlyn was thoroughly disgusted.

19

Ashlyn had finally put her house in order. At least as far as the aesthetics went. The things between Mason and her were still pretty strange in her mind. At times, she felt like she didn't know how to speak with him at all, and it was baffling and sad that she felt like that after so many years of marriage.

After their argument the other evening, Ashlyn had gone back to the documentary to find out about the latest woman who'd gone missing. Her name was Natalie Quinn, and she was an exotic dancer who lived in Tahoe City. Apparently, she went missing a while back, but her employer hadn't reported her disappearance right away. So technically she was the second woman, after Amanda, not the fourth.

When her employer was asked why he'd waited to report her as missing, he basically said that these women came and went, and he couldn't keep track of them at times. However, some of the other girls who knew Natalie had pressured their boss to call the cops because they were worried.

Involving the police was a smart move because now they knew for sure that she was missing.

Ashlyn was very stressed.

She wanted to see Karina since she was concerned about her younger sister. She was a redhead too, no matter that she wore it pretty short these days because she dressed in a punk, rock-and-roll way. She even had a few piercings and a couple of tattoos that their father grumbled about.

Ashlyn invited Karina for coffee, realizing she couldn't have a serious conversation in front of their parents. Ashlyn didn't want to worry Mom and Dad. She knew they didn't watch the news, so there was a good chance that they knew nothing about what was going on.

Mom's prayer group might gossip about it, but since Ashlyn hadn't received a panicked text from her mom, she figured that meant such a subject hadn't come up yet. Jesus Christ always took precedence.

Karina agreed to see her, although it was obvious that she was taken aback by the invite. It had been a while since they'd hung out, just the two of them, and realizing that made Ashlyn sad. She loved her sister dearly, despite their differences, and she wanted to put in an effort and try to mend their strained relationship.

Ashlyn made the drive into the city on high alert. She stayed aware of her surroundings as she drove around the block several times to be sure she didn't pick up that eerie feeling of being followed. So far, she hadn't felt it and she decided it was safe to go into the café and meet her sister. She ordered a latte and then found a table in the corner where she could watch for Karina to arrive.

"So, what's this about? What did I do now?" Karina asked

without even ordering a drink, defensive from the start. She hadn't even sat down when she cut straight to the chase.

Ashlyn knew instantly why her sister behaved this way. In the past, during all the rough periods, Ashlyn always sat her down to have a serious chat, instill some sense in her, and make her see how her behavior was hurting their parents. Not that it ever made any difference. Karina always did what she wanted, regardless.

"You haven't done anything, as far as I'm aware," Ashlyn replied with a smile. "Go order your drink."

Giving her an oddly suspicious look, Karina did as she asked, then returned to the table with her drink and a pastry. "Okay, what is this all about? You don't call me unless you want to rag on me about something."

"Have you been watching the news lately?" Ashlyn asked, sipping her latte.

Her sister made a face. "You know I don't watch that shit."

"Maybe you should start."

Karina looked at her oddly, as though deciding whether Ashlyn had completely lost her mind.

I'm not even sure of that.

"Okay, I'll bite. Why do you think I should start watching the news?"

"Have you heard about the women being kidnapped?"

Karina made a noncommittal gesture. "I think I heard about it around campus. What's that have to do with me? Why are you bringing that up?"

Ashlyn pulled out her phone and showed Karina one of the latest articles about the four women who had gone missing.

Karina started scrolling.

Knowing her sister and how superficial she could be at times, Ashlyn said, "They're all from around here, and they all look like us, so I'm worried."

Karina looked up at her. "They look like us?"

"Yes."

Her sister returned to the article. "Oh, shit. This psychopath has a type," she commented with a laugh.

Ashlyn snatched her phone back because it was clear her sister had finished reading. "Karina, please don't joke about it. This is serious," she chastised. She was having flashbacks to her conversation with Mason. Why wouldn't anyone else take this seriously?

"Why are you so worried? As far as I can see, he only takes younger women," Karina pointed out.

Ashlyn, who was only twenty-eight, took offense to that, but her sister did have a point. The women taken ranged from nineteen to twenty-three. Which was the reason she was trying to get Karina to pay attention, because Karina was twenty-three. "I'm worried about *you*."

"Excuse me?" Karina looked taken aback.

"You're going to all your classes at college, and staying late at times, and I'm concerned about you."

Of course she was more worried about her sister than she was about herself. And not because this maniac apparently had an age preference as well. Ashlyn barely came to town these days, and when she did, it was always in the middle of the day. And while she had been stalked when she was here quite a bit, she knew from the documentary that this predator liked to hunt late at night, so she shouldn't really worry all that much about herself. Karina, on the other hand, liked to party and be out late at night.

Karina took a moment to reply. "I'm genuinely touched,"

she said, placing a hand over Ashlyn's. "I didn't know you cared that much."

Ashlyn was aghast at hearing that. "Of course I care," she replied.

"I know. It was a bad joke," Karina reassured her. "And I appreciate you coming to warn me, but let me tell you something. There's no reason for you to be worried about me."

"Karina..."

"I'm serious, Ash. Thanks to Paul," who was an ex of hers, bad news as far as Ashlyn was concerned, "I learned some pretty gnarly survival skills," she tried to reassure with a wink.

"That doesn't mean you need to test them," Ashlyn pointed out.

"Just chill." Karina was adamant. "I'll be fine."

"Fine. I will. And you don't do anything stupid. Stay safe, please," Ashlyn snapped in return.

Karina smiled. "I will. I promise."

Feeling like she finally got what she came for, Ashlyn nodded. "Good."

After finishing their coffee, they went home so Ashlyn could see her parents. She spent several pleasant hours with them. She felt like her mind got some rest from all the worries, too.

However, on her way home, she caught herself worrying about her baby sister all over again. She was afraid Karina wouldn't take her warnings seriously. She hoped with all her heart that her carefree attitude would not lead her to a world of trouble. After all, that was how she'd met Paul in the first place.

Once she returned home, Ashlyn headed for the kitchen to get dinner started. She was hoping to spend some time with Mason. However, just as she put the water on to boil, Mason called.

"Hey, sweetheart, I just wanted to let you know I'm staying in the city tonight. I've got a big meeting early tomorrow and I don't want to worry about having to drive back here so early."

"All right," she replied, turning off the stove with a sigh. There was no point in making lasagna now. "I guess I'll see you tomorrow night then?"

"Sure. Love you." Mason hung up before she could even reply.

She felt spent, tired of fighting, so she went along with it. Although there was a part of her that wanted to call him back and ask him to come home anyway, she didn't. No matter whether they shared a bed, knowing he was inside the house made all the difference for her and her peace of mind, and that was what she was really concerned about.

She was still a bit fearful of spending a night alone inside the house because that crazy person who'd stabbed her husband was still on the loose. Then again, she was relieved he would be away so she wouldn't have to deal with him. He was not very supportive or sensitive about the subject involving kidnapped women, so it would be best if he was away. Perhaps some alone time would give him clarity, or so she hoped.

What if it doesn't? she worried.

20

After crying herself to sleep twice over the last several days, Ashlyn admitted that she and her husband were once again out of sync. The magical bond they'd formed in New Orleans had not lasted. As she feared, the excitement wore off quickly and they regressed to their old patterns. Especially Mason. She considered the trip to be a step in the right direction, but since there was no follow-up, it had all been for nothing.

She was completely stressed by the state of her marriage and the state of the world around her, and she was afraid to leave the house. Mason was of no help to her. He showed no understanding or compassion toward what she was going through, brushing everything she felt aside. He called her unreasonable and too emotional.

So, she stopped speaking about it with him, right before she stopped speaking with him altogether. But then he would come to make amends. In his way, on his terms, which irked her at times. He was not capable of admitting he was wrong.

Such a control freak could never be wrong, she grumbled.

Like a fool, she would relent because, ultimately, she loved him and was desperate to make their marriage work.

Ashlyn could sense something was wrong. Something was eating at their marriage on a deeper level. She became convinced that Mason was keeping something from her. *Is he cheating? Is that why he is staying over in Tahoe several nights a week now?*

Does he have a mistress?

He always turned off his computer each time she came into his office to speak with him. His phone was out of eyeshot, screen downward, whenever they shared a meal.

He'd also stopped talking with her about his days at work or about his clients, only complaining how tired he was. She could understand that since he barely slept. She knew that because she went to bed alone and woke up alone as well. And there were times when she could see he'd never even come to bed when he was home.

At this point, he could move into his man cave, and she wouldn't know the difference, she thought bitterly.

At first, she thought all this secrecy revolved around their anniversary. That was the last sliver of hope that resided in her, that things still could turn out for the better. That maybe he was just trying to hide some big surprise for her.

But after their latest fight, she wasn't so sure. She'd brought up how she missed him and how she didn't like him staying in Tahoe so much and that even when he was home, he didn't want to spend time with her. He'd told her how she'd changed and that he missed his wife, the one he'd married five years ago.

That hurt her feelings because she didn't feel like she was the one who'd changed.

However, wasn't that one of the signs he was having an affair? Placing blame on her so he wouldn't feel guilty about what he was doing?

Her mind was definitely running wild, creating all kinds of scenarios. Was she not enough for him? Was she lacking something that he needed? Maybe he didn't think it was cheating because he was seeing multiple women? Was that it? Did he have more than one mistress?

She tried to be what he wanted her to be. She made sure not to agitate him, her hair was just the way he liked it, and she always dressed up and prepared a nice meal. But it seemed like she was the only one trying. He wasn't meeting her halfway.

Not to mention, she couldn't track all his mood swings. It was impossible to have a conversation with him when he came home in a bad mood. It hurt her feelings when he walked around as though constantly disappointed with her, even angry with her, while Ashlyn had no idea what she'd done wrong.

When he was home with her at all. And when he was, Mason spent a great deal of time alone in his man cave, avoiding her.

Nothing made sense to her anymore. Not his behavior, not their lives in general. And his insomnia had definitely gotten worse, because he was constantly slipping out of bed —if he even came to bed at all—to go to his man cave in the middle of the night.

She knew that because she'd followed him a couple of times, deluding herself that he was going out to meet his mistress, but so far, she'd never caught him with any other woman. As it turned out, he was cheating on her with his PlayStation. At least as far as she could tell.

Count your blessings, her mother would say.

She couldn't. She was miserable all the time and could feel he was growing more distant each day.

They'd stopped having sex altogether, and Mason had canceled their last date night.

Out of desperation, she tried seducing him one night and was thrilled when it worked. Mason always liked to be in control, no matter what he did, so sex was no different, and although she initiated it, he took charge shortly after.

And then it all changed. They were in the living room, and he flipped her over, pushing her down against the cushions as he pounded into her pretty roughly. His fingers were gripping her arms tightly as he held her down.

Ashlyn was shocked since he had never been like that with her before. She wasn't sure she liked it. The uncertainty didn't last long.

Ashlyn struggled to move away. "You're hurting me." She started to cry out, unable to take it anymore. "Mason," she pleaded.

He let out a sound of pure frustration, almost anger, withdrawing from her. Zipping his pants back up, he turned away from her as she shook in disbelief.

Mason had always been so gentle with her it was hard not to wonder what that was about.

So, she asked, "What just happened, Mason?"

"I was wondering the same thing... I'm sorry. I just thought I'd try something different, but I guess it was too much. I think I'm stressed about work and frustrated with this project. I'm gonna just go try to get my head together." And with that, he left the room.

He went to his man cave and Ashlyn gathered the strength to go to bed. She cried herself to sleep, wondering if it was really work that was bothering him, or if he was secretly mad at her over something and didn't want to tell her.

21

Ashlyn firmly believed that her marriage could be mended if only she put effort into it. When all was said and done, she still loved her husband very much, and she knew the same could be said for him.

But how to fix something when she had no idea how it got broken in the first place? She racked her brain yet came up with nothing.

They needed therapy. Only by talking with an unbiased professional could they find the root of their problems. She'd tried to talk him into it before without any luck, but she couldn't give up hope that he'd want to repair their relationship too.

What if we are beyond repair? she caught herself wondering more than once. Naturally, each time she had that thought, she dismissed it immediately because that was too horrible to comprehend. She couldn't imagine her life without Mason. Despite everything, she didn't want to.

Just because she knew something was wrong and wanted to fix it didn't mean Mason felt the same way. The question was how to make Mason see they needed therapy when she couldn't even communicate simple stuff to him, like having dinner with her parents?

That was how she got the idea. She needed to start slow, and with simple things, not overwhelm him with too much stuff.

Maybe if they socialized a bit more, they would not be so focused on one another all the time, and then maybe the tension between them would ease a bit and Mason would become more open to new ideas. Like therapy, which was the ultimate goal.

It is worth a try. At least, she thought so.

The problem was that Mason wasn't fond of any of her friends. He called them drama makers. Although she would admit that some, especially Stasi, leaned that way, they were not so bad. Regardless, Mason had met with them only a handful of times, and she couldn't see that changing. They had nothing in common except for her.

That left her family as a way of enriching their social lives. Mason was pretty clear on what he thought of them as well. He didn't like spending time with them. He only did so after massive pressure was put on him.

Come to think of it, he hadn't even spent time with them when he'd flown them to Hawaii so they could attend the wedding. Apart from the ceremony and one dinner afterward, they went their separate ways. At the time, it felt natural to her because they'd just gotten married and were on their honeymoon, but now she wondered if Mason had acted like that because he didn't like them, even back then.

What was she supposed to do?

Ask to hang out with his friends? She wasn't sure he had

any. He had plenty of colleagues and business associates whom he saw frequently, went to lunches, and played softball with, but Ashlyn suspected that was all work-related as well.

Was it weird that she only now realized her husband had no real friends that she knew of? He had a lot of connections, people he networked with, worked with at the agency, and of course there were clients, but no one she would say he was close to.

He worked a lot, so it was understandable that he had no time for forming such friendly relationships. Besides, he always said he loved spending all his free time with her. When had that changed?

Not dwelling on that, she refocused on the problem at hand. Realizing she had a better chance convincing him to have dinner with her parents than with some of her friends, she wasted no time in setting everything up.

She knew her mother would have no objections to adding an additional plate to Sunday dinner, so it was all about convincing Mason to attend.

Over the course of a few days, whenever she got the opportunity, she would hint at how she missed her parents and how it would be lovely for them to sit together and share a meal, like a family, and share impressions about their trip to New Orleans. Which she never got an opportunity to do because of the whole incident with the intruder and Mason getting wounded.

"Mostly, I want to brag about this," she concluded, flashing her new diamond ring.

In return, Mason grumbled something completely incoherently.

She understood the gist. He was not pleased. That was

why she used the ultimate weapon. "Or we can always invite them here. I would love to test our new kitchen."

"No, you're right. We should go visit them," he agreed, somewhat grudgingly.

Ashlyn was dancing with joy inside her head because she felt like this was a huge victory. At the same time, she completely ignored what it said about Mason that he didn't want his in-laws around.

Before the big event, Ashlyn sent a whole box of food to her parents' house. When her mother called to ask what that was about, threatening to send it back, Ashlyn said there had been a mix-up with the deliveries.

"I didn't get a chance to use all the products that they sent previously, and since it would be such a waste to throw it away, I sent it to you. It was free of charge, anyway," she added as though in afterthought, knowing that would help her mother come to terms with the fact that Ashlyn had just sent her a month's worth of provisions.

"Well, it would be such a waste," her mom agreed like Ashlyn knew she would. In her mind, there was no greater sin than wasting food. "Thank you."

"No problem," Ashlyn replied, finishing the conversation after hinting that Mason might drop by for dinner as well.

Her mother was pleased to hear that, naturally. She was kind hearted. No matter what, she saw the good in people. Ashlyn always strived to be like her, yet she wasn't so sure she was succeeding. And she hated lying to her, as she had now. Although it was necessary, because her mother, and especially her father, were too proud to accept help at times. And Ashlyn was in a position to help.

She knew they were not starving, but she always felt like she could do so much more to help. Unfortunately, over time, she had to settle for making sure they ate something healthy for a change.

On Sunday, Mason stayed in his office so late that part of her was convinced he was about to cancel dinner. Luckily, he didn't, which she took as a great sign. Like her, he was putting in effort. That was what marriage was all about—compromises. Sometimes, he did what she wanted, and other times, she did what he wanted.

"Which one of these do you think I should wear, green or navy?" she asked her husband for an opinion to distract herself.

Mason shrugged. "Don't make a fuss. We're only going to see your parents."

"I still want to look good."

"You always look good, my love." He smiled, and it reminded her of how he used to be with her, how he used to look at her.

"Thank you, but that doesn't help me to decide."

"All right, wear the navy. You look lovely in it." He pointed at the dress on the right.

"Thank you," she replied with a smile, returning the other inside the closet.

"I don't want us to be late, so if you could finish up quickly, I'd appreciate it," he urged before returning downstairs.

Ashlyn rushed to change before joining him. He was right. It would be rude to be late, especially since she wanted to help with dinner. Her mom would refuse, fussing, but eventually would allow her to contribute. It was part of the dance, part of their routine, and at times Ashlyn missed it.

The ride to her parents' house was long and silent. Ashlyn tried engaging him a couple of times, but it seemed like he wasn't in the mood to talk to her. Actually, he looked miles away, as though something else was on his mind.

Is that movie star client still bothering him? she wondered.

Figuring it must be something work-related, she let him be. Besides, she didn't want to agitate him right before having dinner with her parents. She wanted this night to go well. She needed that.

Here we go, she thought before Mason knocked on the door. No matter how many times she told him they could just go inside, he wouldn't allow it.

Maybe part of the reason he always feels like a guest is because he behaves like one, she thought.

Her dad opened the door.

"Good evening, Mr. Dawson," Mason addressed him formally.

"Good evening, Mason," her dad countered in the same manner.

The first encounter was strained, as it always was, and it didn't improve with time.

Ashlyn's mother fussed over Mason, treating him like royalty or the Pope. Her father practically ignored him, engaged in conversation with him only once.

Karina and Mason shared an animosity, and Ashlyn hoped they wouldn't make a scene. Ashlyn had spoken with Karina beforehand, pleading with her not to start an argument, and although she hadn't actually promised, she did say she would do her best. Actually, she'd said she would act in Ashlyn's best interests. For Karina, that was huge, and Ashlyn appreciated the effort.

She hoped all would be on their best behavior because she wanted to show her husband that he was wrong about her family. Yet her family and their ways were not the only problem. Mason wasn't trying to get to know them, either.

For the first time since she'd married him, she got to see what others saw in him. That arrogant side of him that believed he was so much better than everyone else.

She noticed it right from the moment they entered her parents' home. She saw how he eyed the old furniture with disdain. She saw the contempt about her mother's modest Sunday best, the frown when he regarded the table set with old china. It was a set her mother was extremely proud of since it had been in their family for generations. It was an honor that her mother allowed it to be used that night, for that dinner, for him, and Mason either overlooked that fact or didn't care. All he saw was modesty, although he would use a different word—poverty.

The gap between their wealth was huge, yet the one between the people gathered to share a meal was even greater.

For the first time, Ashlyn was aware of that and realized how foolish she was to force this farce on anyone. Because now she knew her husband would never change. He would never stop regarding her parents in a certain way, just as her mother and father wouldn't stop seeing Mason their way.

I've made a terrible mistake.

Then they all sat down to have dinner. It hadn't even started, and she already wanted it over. Apparently, each person shared that sentiment.

Trying to lighten the mood, Ashlyn attempted to engage them in conversation, and the infuriating thing was that no one was cooperating. Her mom was constantly in and out of the kitchen, her father sat so he could watch the game on the

TV in the living room, and Karina stared at Mason with open disdain.

This is a disaster. She even started praying out of desperation. *Please, God, help me tonight.*

In her madness, she'd looked at this dinner as an indicator that she and Mason could work it out and stay married. So she needed this to work.

"We had a nice time in New Orleans," Ashlyn chatted mostly to herself.

"So, tell me, Mason," Karina said, completely unexpectedly, cutting her off, "is being a heartless bastard a course they taught you in Harvard, or is that something you were born with?"

Ashlyn almost bit off her tongue. And she heard her mother dropping something in the kitchen as her father smirked. This was one of the rare times daughter and father agreed on something.

The situation became tense, but Mason looked at Karina and smiled. "I went to Yale," he corrected.

"I'm so sorry, Mason," her mother said, clearly mortified that her daughter had insulted him. "I don't know where Karina misplaced her manners."

Mason gracefully shook his head as though he didn't mind. Ashlyn knew he did. She could see it in his eyes.

Karina knew as well. "Mom, please don't apologize for me. Besides, I have plenty of questions for him. He rarely visits. I want to catch up."

Her mom looked flustered, but her dad was amused and finally engaged in dinner.

Ashlyn was stunned. She had no idea what was going on or how to react.

"Please, ask whatever you like," Mason countered, showing a lot of teeth.

"Why are you here?" Karina asked without a pause.

"Excuse me?" Mason looked taken aback.

"You clearly hate us. Most of the time, I'm not sure you even like Ashlyn, considering how you treat her. So, let me ask again. Why are you here? To show us how much better you are than us?"

The dinner was officially over since they'd all stopped eating. It seemed everyone was expecting Mason's reply. Ashlyn included.

"She lives in a house I built for her like a queen. She wants for nothing." *Apart from you.* "So, how do I mistreat her, exactly?"

"You treat her poorly, like a bad husband would, otherwise she wouldn't be so miserable all the time, crying to us."

"I don't—" Ashlyn started to defend herself and Mason.

"Karina, that's enough." Her mother tried again to end this, but there was no stopping this train wreck.

"Not nearly enough," Karina argued. "Maybe all of you are too scared to say anything, but I'm not. Someone has to tell him the truth."

"And you should start minding your own business," Mason snapped in return.

"My sister is my business."

"No, she is mine," Mason insisted, "and someone around here needs to tell you to get your shit together and learn your place."

"Finally, the asshole reveals his true face."

"Only to uppity bitches like yourself."

"Mason, that's enough," Ashlyn said, standing up. She couldn't believe he'd said that to her sister. "We're leaving."

And the real indicator of how things stood was seen in the fact that nobody tried to stop them, not even her kindhearted mother, as they walked out the door.

Ashlyn was reeling. She couldn't believe what had just happened.

She'd wanted one night, one night with all the people she loved, eating together in peace, but apparently, that was too much to ask.

As she closed the car door behind her, the bang reverberated with something deep inside her and she snapped. "How could you embarrass me in front of my parents like that?" She genuinely felt betrayed.

Mason gave her a sulky look. "She started it."

"Oh, don't give me that. You're the older one. You should mind your temper."

"Me? Your sister attacked me," he yelled in return.

"Right, she did, and I'm just as mad at her. However, it was clear from the start that you didn't want to be there. You were judging everything and everyone."

"Of course I was judging. I can't believe those people are your family. They are beneath us, Ashlyn, and this dinner proved that. And don't even get me started on your tobacco-smelling, tattoo-covered trainwreck of a sister. Someone should teach her some manners. You should be grateful I rescued you from being so low-class like the rest of them."

"Wow," she replied, calmer than she was, controlling the tears just waiting to spill over. She was not going to cry, not here, not now, and definitely not in front of him. She had her pride. "I'm glad I finally know exactly how you feel." Saying that, she turned her head away from him to look through the windows.

Mason started the car and drove them straight home.

Home. How cruel that sounded.

Treating her like a queen. *Yeah, right.* She felt regal, especially now. *What a joke.*

When they arrived, they entered the house and started walking upstairs without saying a word.

Ashlyn stopped midway. "I need a break from our relationship."

"What does that mean? Are you leaving me?" He looked more rattled now than he'd been during dinner.

Some small part of her was glad.

"Not yet, but I need space. I don't want to sleep in the same bed as you anymore." She couldn't bear it, after all she'd heard tonight.

Mason narrowed his eyes. "You're blackmailing me with this to try and gain control of our relationship."

She took a step toward him. "In this marriage, I'm definitely not the one obsessed with control," she threw in his face before resuming the climb up the stairs.

They went their separate ways. Ashlyn went to the bedroom, and Mason chose one of the guestrooms to sleep in.

Ashlyn half-thought he might come to her, apologetic, sincere, and wanting to repair things, but he stayed away, and she cried into her pillow until she finally fell asleep.

22

Ashlyn had cried herself to sleep, never imagining that her marriage would fall apart as it had been over the last several months. This was supposed to be the best time of their lives and now she feared it was all over. How could Mason treat her, treat her family in such a way? She was devastated.

After getting dressed for the day, she went downstairs and was startled to see Mason in the kitchen, cooking her favorite pancakes. She stood in the doorway silent, her arms crossed as she stared at him. The table was set with a nice tablecloth, a vase of flowers as its centerpiece. Was he trying to gaslight her? Make her think last night hadn't happened?

"What are you doing?" she asked, her voice harsh and untrusting.

Mason turned and glanced at her. His face was a mask of contrition. "I'm apologizing. What happened last night shouldn't have. I should have held my temper and not let your sister goad me. I should have been more polite to your parents. It's just... I know they don't like me, and I've been having a hard time with work lately and it all just sort of got to me." He turned back to the pan and flipped one of the hot cakes.

Ashlyn frowned. It had felt like more happened than just that, but maybe this was a step in the right direction? Could she trust it though? Mason had done this before. Blown up, said stuff he shouldn't have, thought things that he shouldn't have, but then apologized, as though that made everything all right.

"They don't like you because you clearly don't like them. You called them trash, Mason," Ashlyn stuck to her guns. She was done allowing him to just skate through things and not answer for the awful things he's said.

"I know. I'm sorry. It wasn't really personal. I mean, it's just how they act. How they don't seem to want to better themselves, and how they stay perpetually in the same mindset that bothers me. I try not to let it get to me, but it does. Especially after—" He stopped and pulled the pancakes off the skillet, plating them. "Look, I know you love them, and that's great, but they don't like me. They don't like the kind of life we have. They always think the worst of me. I can't promise that their hatred toward me won't get to me, sweetheart. But I will try not to let it affect us. I love you and all I want is for you to be happy."

Ashlyn didn't know what to think. In a way, his words were everything she needed to hear, but then he was still mostly blaming them for how he reacted and that didn't seem right either. Yes, she was mad at Karina too for starting everything, but something about his apology seemed as though it wasn't actually an apology. More of an excuse for his behavior.

"Do you forgive me?" he asked as he set the plate of

stacked pancakes on the table along with the bottle of syrup. He turned and moved toward Ashlyn, his arms wide, as though he wanted to hug her, but he stopped short right in front of her. "Please?"

Again, she didn't quite know what to do. She wanted to forgive him. She wanted to move on from last night, but something in her held her back. There was still something very wrong in their marriage and she didn't want to just dismiss those feelings. She tried to formulate words to express what she was feeling, but was coming up short.

"Ashlyn, please. I promise, I won't let it happen again."

Ashlyn shook her head. "I appreciate you apologizing to me, but I'm not the only one who deserves an apology from you. And this isn't all just about last night. You've been... distant. Callous, and dismissive of me for a while now. There's something wrong in our marriage, Mason. There has been since we moved into this house. Anytime you don't like something I have to say, you run away to your man cave and hide from me."

"I know. I'm sorry. I've not been handling things well. Work has been keeping me stressed and I haven't been very open about it with you. I'll change that if I have to." He glanced over his shoulder at the table. "What do you say? Will you forgive me and come eat with me?"

"I do forgive you, but things need to change, Mason. I think we need to go to couples' counseling, and you need to apologize to my family."

Mason made a face at her demands, but didn't say anything immediately.

Ashlyn bit her tongue, and seeing he was going to continue to stonewall her on the topic of counseling and apologizing to her family, she turned on her heel and left the room.

"Ashlyn, wait. Please. Yes, of course I will go to counseling if that's what it's going to take. I just don't know when I'm going to have the time—" He'd followed her into the hall.

Ashlyn whirled back around. "If I'm that important to you, then you'll make the time."

"Right, of course, you're right. We'll make the time. I just need you to forgive me." He gave her a pleading look.

"And you'll apologize to Karina? To my parents? You'll make an effort with them?"

He pressed his lips together for a moment, and he almost looked mutinous, but then he nodded. "Yes, of course. I'll stop by there today, after work. I promise."

For the first time since last night, Ashlyn felt herself relaxing. She was feeling extremely stressed about everything and now she could see some hope coming into her life. A light at the end of the very dark tunnel they'd been in. She just hoped he was being sincere. "Okay, I forgive you, if you're serious about the counseling and your promise."

"I am. In fact, I will start looking for a counselor today." He wrapped his arms around her and pulled her close.

"You don't have to do that. I can—" Ashlyn started to tell him she would find a proper counselor, but he stopped her.

"No, no. I caused this friction between us with my behavior. Let me fix it."

Ashlyn liked that he was taking responsibility for everything that had happened and decided to allow him to do it. She nodded as they moved back toward the kitchen.

"And while I'm doing that, I've booked you a spa day at High Valley Spa."

Ashlyn was taken aback. "What? A spa day? I don't need—"

"It's my special treat for you, for putting up with me. Part of my apology." He smiled and kissed her temple. "Let's eat these hot cakes, which probably aren't so hot anymore, and then you can go get ready."

Smiling, she realized he was trying to be thoughtful, and she agreed. "Okay. Thank you," she said tentatively. She wasn't quite sure she trusted him to do what she wanted but she was willing to give him the benefit of the doubt for now. After all, they'd been married for five years, and she loved him. She needed to believe that they could get back to where they were prior to the move.

"Your appointment is for eleven," Mason shared as they started to eat. "So you've got plenty of time to eat before you go. Unfortunately, I can't wait to drive you into town. I've got a meeting at ten with that celebrity again. None of the designs I've done have been to their liking."

"Is this the same client you've been dealing with for a while?"

Mason nodded. "Yes. I thought we had it all worked out, but at the last minute, they completely changed their mind and wanted to start over from scratch. They've been a nightmare."

And just like that, Ashlyn understood how much stress Mason had been under lately. It made it so much easier to accept his apology because of that. "You know you can always talk to me, Mason. When you're stressed like that. You don't have to keep it all bottled up inside."

"I know, my love. I'm just used to dealing with that sort of thing on my own." Mason finished his food and then took his plate to the sink. "I'd better go. I'll see you tonight, all right?"

Ashlyn smiled. "Of course. And you'll look up counselors today?"

"I will. I can't promise I'll book one yet, but I'll look into them."

It was enough for the moment. "Thank you." Ashlyn smiled and allowed him to help her up from her chair.

He took her into his arms and kissed her properly.

"Good luck today."

"Thank you, my love. I'll see you later." Mason grabbed his keys from the counter, headed for his office where he picked up his briefcase and then, with a wave, headed for the garage.

Watching him leave, Ashlyn couldn't help but feel things were looking up. She went upstairs and dressed, then, with a glance at the clock, decided she would swing by her parents' house and talk to Karina before her appointment.

She made the hour-long drive into the city and pulled up to the house. Neither of her parents' cars were in the drive, though. Still, she went to the door and knocked.

A moment later the door swung open, and Karina stood there. "Did you leave him, or did he kick you out?"

"What? No. Why would you think that?" Ashlyn frowned at her sister.

"You saw how he acted last night. The man is an asshole."

Gritting her teeth, Ashlyn glared at her sister. "He might have behaved like an asshole last night, but you were being a bitch. And I'll have you know he apologized and is going to go to counseling with me. He's just been under a lot of stress at work."

"Whatever. Once an asshole, always an asshole. Why are you here? Trying to brag?"

"No. I'm—" Ashlyn stopped. There was no getting through to her sister. "Look, Mason said he's coming by here after work to apologize to you and Mom and Dad. Just be nice, okay?"

Karina shrugged. "We'll see."

Ashlyn shook her head. She didn't know why she bothered. "I've got to go. I've got an appointment." As she headed toward the door, she paused. "You're still staying safe, right? Not going out at night?"

Karina just smirked.

Ashlyn stared at her sister. "Karina—"

"Save it. I'm a big girl, Ashlyn. I can take care of myself." Karina swung the door open, as though dismissing her.

Knowing she couldn't control what her sister did, Ashlyn returned to her car. As she got in, she had that feeling again of being watched. Looking about, she noticed a white van parked down the street. She couldn't make out the plate number from where she was, but something about it gave her the creeps. Shivering, she backed out of the driveway, into the street and headed away from the van. She couldn't be sure the feeling of being watched came from the van itself, but once she was out of the neighborhood, she felt better and more normal.

Smiling, she entered the spa and was delighted to find that Mason had booked her for several treatments, starting with an hour-long massage. By the time she left four hours later, she'd had a massage, a facial, her bikini-line waxed, and a mani-pedi.

When she got home, she started making lasagna so it

would be ready for when Mason got home. She was anxious to see how his apology to her parents and Karina went and to find out if he'd actually called around to find them a counselor.

23

Ashlyn was woken up by a phone call. Glancing at the clock, she realized she had overslept since it was close to one p.m. She'd barely slept last night. After a very late dinner, Mason had kept her up, making love to her for half the night, so it was no wonder. She had no idea if he'd managed to get any sleep at all before he'd left for an early morning meeting around four a.m. this morning.

Still feeling kind of groggy, without bothering to read who was trying to reach her, she answered.

"Hello?" Her voice sounded off to her own ears.

"Ashlyn, thank God." Her mother's panicky voice chased the remnants of sleep away. "I've been trying to reach you for hours."

She had? She must have been pretty out of it if she hadn't heard the phone before.

"What happened?" Ashlyn demanded, knowing something must have occurred, otherwise her mother wouldn't sound like this.

"It's Karina."

Ashlyn rubbed her eyes, sitting up. They'd had too many conversations starting like this in the past. Karina must have gotten herself arrested or something, she hypothesized. Lord knew it wouldn't be the first time.

"What did she do?"

"She went out last night and never came home," her mother explained.

"She went out at night after I specifically told her not to?" Ashlyn asked rhetorically, getting angry. There was a kidnapper on the loose, preying on women who looked like her, yet here she was, acting like a brat.

"You know how she gets. She was in a mood after Mason stopped by with his apologies. She said she was going out to buy cigarettes, maybe have a drink."

Their father didn't allow her to smoke inside the house. It was the reason for many arguments inside their household.

"She doesn't need a whole night for that," Ashlyn argued, although she couldn't fully understand why. It wasn't her mother's fault that Karina was acting like an idiot.

"I'm very worried, Ashlyn."

So was she. Flashes of that white van in her parents' neighborhood flitted through her mind. Was it the kidnapper? Had they targeted Karina? Fear swept through Ashlyn.

Still, she couldn't jump to that conclusion. Maybe Karina was just out being Karina. "Maybe she's with one of her friends," Ashlyn provided.

"She stopped seeing those people when she started going to classes."

That was true. Karina *had* cut all ties with all her friends while she was trying to turn her life around, and Ashlyn knew that. But maybe she'd made some new friends. "Do you know if she's made any new ones? I mean friends from her college maybe?"

"No, I don't think so. Not that she's talked about anyway."

Ashlyn grew even more worried. "Did you call the police?" she asked, frowning.

"No, not yet," her mother replied, startled.

"Call them now," Ashlyn urged. "Make sure you explicitly say she is a redhead." She couldn't shake the idea that the kidnapper had gotten to her. This was what she'd been worried about all along.

"What? Why?" her mother asked, confirming to Ashlyn that she knew nothing about what was going on in the city.

"Just do as I say. I'm on my way."

Hanging up, Ashlyn dressed and practically ran out of the house. She dialed Mason's number on the way to her car, but then recalled he was going to be in meetings all day and hung up. He couldn't help right now, and she didn't want to put any more stress on him. As she drove through the security gate, Ashlyn couldn't stop the thoughts running through her mind about her sister having been kidnapped.

Her baby sister might be in danger. *Oh, Karina.* Ashlyn tried hard not to think about what might be happening to her right now.

Why did she have to go out in the middle of the night? She knew why. It was because Mason had stopped by. He'd said everything went fine, but had it? She hadn't called Karina to check in with her. What if Mason had said or done something to piss Karina off more?

Oh, Karina, please be well, she prayed with all her might.

Part of her expected to see her in the house once she

drove there. Unfortunately, she arrived just in time to see the police patrol car driving away.

What did happen? she wondered, rushing inside the house.

"Ashlyn," her mother cried out, clearly in distress.

Ashlyn instantly went to hug her. Glancing about, she saw her father sitting on the couch, expression grave as he watched the TV. She knew that was all for show. He was rattled as well.

"Everything will be all right, Mom," she tried to comfort as they parted. "What happened? I saw the police driving away."

"I did as you said, and they instantly came to get her picture. Ashlyn, what is going on?"

"Didn't they explain anything to you?"

"*No.*" Her mother stressed the word. It was obvious how confused, upset, flustered, and scared she was.

Bless her heart for not watching the news. Ashlyn had a fleeting thought. "Let's all sit down," she urged.

"Ashlyn, you're scaring me."

Ashlyn bit her tongue to not say how scared she was as well.

"Tell us what is going on," her father decided to speak up as well. "Did she get involved with something?"

"No, this isn't her fault," Ashlyn defended instantly.

"Then what is it?" her father said gruffly.

She realized she should just tell them, fast and without sugarcoating. *Like ripping off a Band-Aid.* "There's a serial kidnapper on the loose. And he only takes women who look like me and Karina, redheads with green eyes. That doesn't have to mean anything," she was quick to add, not being able to completely break her parents' hearts. "There's still a chance she's sleeping off a hangover at a friend's house."

"I tried calling her all day long. She's unavailable," her mom countered.

"There is someone kidnapping redheads?" her father repeated.

Ashlyn nodded.

"A killer?"

"Nobody knows at this point," Ashlyn replied honestly.

Her father got red in the face before storming out of the room.

"No, please, God, not my baby." Her mother started to cry.

"Everything will be all right, Mom. The police are involved. They'll find her."

She stayed with her parents the rest of the day, waiting for any kind of news. There was none. And when they watched the news, nobody mentioned Karina.

As they approached the evening, she tried to convince her mother to eat something.

Her dad completely lost patience. While muttering something about the incompetence of the police, he stormed out of the house.

"Brandon, where are you going?" her mother called after him, but he didn't respond.

Ashlyn ran out after him. "Where are you going?" she demanded, catching up with him. "Mom needs you."

"I'm going to the sheriff's department to see if there's any news, and if they haven't managed to find my daughter, I will go look for her myself," he said all in one breath.

It was hard seeing her father like this. Usually, he was pretty stoic and rarely showed emotions, so it was obvious this was hitting him hard. Then again, they all felt the same way.

"Call if you learn anything."

He nodded. "Of course."

Ashlyn returned to the house. At some point, she saw a missed call from Mason and tried to call him back. However, the call simply went to voicemail, and she left a message, letting him know what was going on.

Later that evening, her father finally returned home, and Ashlyn knew he had no good news to share. The beer on his breath suggested as much.

"What happened, Brandon?" her mom demanded.

"It's all true, Melissa, what Ashlyn said."

"Where is my baby?" her mom said, raising her voice.

Ashlyn barely managed to calm her down, but that didn't last, especially with her father coming in like this.

"The police found a security camera video from a bank. On it was Karina, and she was being pushed into an unmarked white van by a man."

Ashlyn closed her eyes. *Oh, no.*

"What man?"

"They believe it's the same man who took the others."

"No." Her mother started to cry, and her father embraced her.

It was pure agony, watching her parents go through this. That maniac had taken their daughter, and there was nothing Ashlyn could do.

Eventually, she gave her mother something to calm down, and the poor woman fell asleep.

As she slept, Ashlyn found her father on the patio. He wiped away the tears as she approached.

"I don't know what to do, Ashlyn. I'm her father, and I don't know how to help my daughter."

"We'll find her, Dad." Ashlyn was adamant.

He nodded, as though too distraught to speak.

"Mom fell asleep," she provided, not being able to withstand the silence anymore.

"Good, good," he was quick to say, dabbing at his eyes again.

Ashlyn hugged him.

"How did this happen? Who took my girl?" Although it was obvious those questions weren't meant for her, she still answered.

"I don't know, but we'll find her." *And make this maniac pay.* Ashlyn would do everything in her power to get her back.

Because there was no alternative.

"We'll find her," she repeated, hugging her dad with all her might.

24

Ashlyn was sitting in the living room, biting her nails, waiting for Mason to arrive home.

He'd called her the night before to tell her that he would be staying late at work and sleeping in the office. He'd also told her he'd gotten her message about Karina being missing, but had merely said she would probably turn up. Ashlyn hadn't been thrilled with his dismissiveness over Karina's disappearance, but she knew he didn't have the same connection to Karina that she did.

Leaving her parents alone for the night was hard, but her mom had convinced her that she should return home to rest, and so she did. On her way home, she tried calling Mason again to give him an update and he didn't answer. She'd known he was working, but with everything going on, she'd hoped he'd answer when she called.

Perhaps it was irrational, but his not answering made her angry. Here she was, needing him the most, and he couldn't even bother to pick up her call. That was why she waited in the living room for him. She wanted to hear his explanation for what kept him away. What was so important that he couldn't speak with his wife for two minutes? Was his work seriously more important than she was?

Her sister was missing, and she needed his support. Support he apparently couldn't bother to give. It didn't matter that he disliked her sister. He should still be there to help her and her family. To comfort them in their hour of need.

The fear for her sister and the fact that Mason was never home created such a whirlwind of emotions that Ashlyn felt like exploding.

She was resentful. The fact that he was never home had to mean something, right? The fact he was never there for her when she really needed him meant he didn't really care, didn't it? There was only one conclusion she could come up with. He was definitely having an affair. It was the only explanation. A proper husband who cared about her would have dropped everything and come to her aid when she needed it, but Mason hadn't. He'd not only been dismissive, he'd stayed gone overnight. She wasn't important enough for him to come help. So he had to have someone else in his life who was.

The thought broke Ashlyn's heart. However, her marital problems had to take a back seat considering all her attention had to be on finding Karina. She would have to deal with Mason's infidelity later.

She'd spent the entire day back in Tahoe with her parents trying to keep them calm as she thought about where her sister could possibly be. The police had taken down names of all Karina's former boyfriends and friends, and so far, they'd heard nothing. It was the lack of communication that bothered her.

After dinner with her parents she'd once again returned home with hopes of catching Mason and finding out why he was once again being distant and unhelpful.

Hearing his car pulling up the drive, she looked at the clock and scoffed. *Lord have mercy, he finally arrives*, she thought sarcastically, bracing herself for another fight.

"Hello, my love," he greeted from the hall. "I've already eaten with a boring-as-fuck client, so I'll be downstairs to unwind. This was a long day."

"You should hear about mine then," she blurted out before she could stop herself as she followed him toward his man cave.

"Later," he said over his shoulder.

His behavior, so dismissive, so cold, irked her. Despite the anger she felt for him and fear for her sister, Ashlyn didn't fail to notice that he hadn't come in to properly greet her. He wasn't interested in hearing about her day.

It was clear that Mason only cared about himself and how to take care of his own needs. His going to his man cave the second he arrived home was clear proof.

She'd started to hate that place and wanted to set it on fire.

Had he always been like this? She dismissed that thought, not allowing herself to get sidetracked.

She would not let him off the hook so easily. Not tonight. Tonight, she would demand answers.

"Wait. I have to tell you something," she practically yelled as he put his hand on the doorknob.

"What is it?" he asked, leaning against the door, looking at her as though tired and impatient to be done with her.

"Didn't you see that I've been calling you all day? Why didn't you answer?" she demanded.

"You know I was in meetings with important clients all day, Ashlyn," he deflected. "I couldn't stop them to take silly calls from my wife."

"Mason, this is serious."

"I told you I was in meetings," he replied, not bothering to provide any more information.

"Why didn't you call me back?"

He straightened up, looking at her oddly, as though not expecting that she would raise her voice. "What's gotten into you? Are you that desperate for another fight that you would start attacking me for no reason?"

"I needed you, and you couldn't bother to speak with me," Ashlyn said, getting up from the couch. "You haven't even asked me about Karina!"

"I already told you I was busy."

"Too busy for your wife while her whole world is crashing down."

"Oh, please, don't be so melodramatic. It's not a good look on you."

"Karina is missing, and I needed you. We all did."

"What are you talking about?" He shook his head and held up a hand to stop her from answering that. "What I mean is, are you sure she's actually missing and not just off at one of her loser boyfriend's?"

"Yes!" Ashlyn shouted in exasperation. "The police found video footage of her being kidnapped!"

"When?" he wanted to know.

Ashlyn thought about it, then said, "The night before last, and you've not been here," she pointed out.

"I'm sorry, my love. As I said before, work has been crazy, and I've been in meetings. I didn't think she was actually kidnapped," he started to defend himself.

"I'm not talking about just tonight, or even when it happened," Ashlyn started, her mind racing. "I'm talking about since you were attacked. You've been so distant, and we keep fighting, and now my sister's missing and you acted like it was no big deal. I told you before about my worries about this kidnapper and you dismissed me about it."

Mason frowned. "I'm sorry. I should have listened, but you have to admit, your sister has always engaged in risky behavior."

Ashlyn gritted her teeth. "Are you kidding me right now? You're blaming her? She went out for cigarettes and to get a drink! She wasn't walking the street like a hooker!"

"Are you sure?"

His words made her beyond furious. Ashlyn wanted to hit something, preferably him.

"Someone took my sister, and you're standing here calling her a whore! I can't believe you!"

"Calm down. I didn't mean that. I meant are you sure that was what she was doing? Going out for a simple drink and cigarettes? You were the one who brought up hooking, not me."

"You're being obtuse!" Ashlyn felt tears stinging her eyes. "Where were you when I needed you?" she demanded.

"When? The night she went missing?"

She meant throughout this entire debacle, not just that night, but then something made her say, "*Yes.*" She stressed the word.

"I'd had a long day of meetings and more in the morning. I told you I was staying at the office." He stared at her for a moment with suspicion. "What are you accusing me of, Ashlyn?"

Ashlyn shook her head. She didn't want to give voice to

her fears that he was cheating on her, but she was so angry at him.

He took a step toward her. "I'm sorry I wasn't here for you, but you know my work is important to me. Are you seriously going to act like this when you know I do all of this for you?"

That was a joke. He didn't work because of her. He could retire right now, and they'd still have millions, he was that rich. No. Mason worked for Mason. "Mason, I'm not doing this with you now."

"What?"

"Talking about our marriage. I'm too worried about Karina. I'm upset you weren't here when I needed you."

"I'm sure the police are doing everything in their power to find her."

"Yeah, like they found all the rest," she snapped in return.

"I don't understand what you want from me. What do you want me to say?"

"I want you to tell me you'll help find her," she insisted.

"Me? How am I supposed to do that? I'm not a cop, Ashlyn."

"I can't believe you." She stared at him, feeling like he was betraying her.

"I know you're upset about Karina, but don't take it out on me," he replied in the same manner.

Ashlyn felt like he'd punched her in the gut. He would stop at nothing to win an argument.

"Oh, you can bet I'm upset—terrified even—that someone kidnapped my sister. However, I'm also distraught because of the fact that my husband is never around, especially when I need him. Because your needs are always more important than mine."

"Here it is, always saying I don't put you first in my life. I do, Ashlyn. It's not my fault if you can't see it."

"What? Did you just seriously say that to me after I informed you that Karina has been kidnapped, and I needed you, but you ignored me! You would rather be with someone else than show a sliver of compassion and give comfort to me?" Ashlyn countered, completely losing her temper.

"You know what? For both our sakes, I'm leaving now. You clearly need to cool off. Because the things you're saying are completely insane."

"Mason, do not dare walk away. I demand answers."

"And I demand some peace and quiet in my fucking house after a long fucking day." And with that, he actually left, yanking open the door to his man cave and slamming it behind him.

"Son of a bitch," she screamed, cursing, which she rarely did, as he left her alone. Ashlyn was so beyond furious, so beyond angry, she felt like she could tear this whole house down with that sheer energy alone.

She couldn't believe him. True, it took two to fight, but he was the one who made things worse. Mason had left and retreated to his damn man cave instead of comforting her and apologizing for not being with her during all of this. She'd wanted his assurance that he would help her find her sister. Why couldn't he see that? Why couldn't he just help her?

It was no secret that Mason and Karina didn't particularly like one another, but this was beyond cold.

The worst part? She didn't believe a word that left his mouth. There probably were no meetings, no dinners with clients. She was sure he was having an affair, so each time he called her his love or sweetheart felt like a dagger through her heart.

That was a definite first, her not trusting him, and she didn't care for the sentiment one bit. She missed the days when all was well between them. Yet having such thoughts was completely useless.

Her sister was missing, so the only thing she could think about was how to bring her back.

Yet the urge to know the truth and discover what was going on with Mason wouldn't leave her alone. Perhaps the stress of the situation was making her act irrationally. Her sister was missing, and she was worried, but since there was nothing that she could do about it but fear where she was and what that man was doing to her, her mind found an escape.

That meant stressing about Mason and his possible mistress. Finding out about the other woman was definitely something she could do. So, she would do some amateur snooping to see what was going on and how long this bastard had been lying to her.

Simultaneously, she would help the police in any way to find Karina. She knew she and her family would have to be vigilant, because a lot of women had disappeared, and the police still had no real leads.

Maybe I should hire a PI to look into Karina's disappearance and make Mason pay for it. That thought almost made her smile. It would be divine justice to do something like that after the way he'd behaved.

25

Once again, Ashlyn and Mason slept in separate beds, and she was glad. She was so angry that she didn't want to share space with him. It especially irked her that he was apparently in a good mood.

That hurt, since it showed her that he didn't care that she was in pain. He didn't care that her family was going through something horrific. Mason looked completely unbothered. She even caught him humming leaving his man cave.

Heartless bastard, she grumbled.

That and more was what kept her awake at night. She couldn't sleep no matter what. Ashlyn constantly expected that her mom would call her to share that Karina had been found, alive or...

She stopped herself.

She couldn't think like that. The police would find her sister safe and sound. And Ashlyn would do her best to help out in any way.

She even came up with the craziest plan to offer herself to the police to act as bait. She was a redhead, after all, and that could be interesting for this kidnapper. The only thing she had to do was allow him to take her away while the police traced her every move, and after reaching all the rest, they could arrest him. It sounded simple inside her head.

Her parents didn't think so. Her father actually threatened to lock her up in her former room if she ever mentioned something like that again.

"We've already lost one daughter. I'm not taking risks with the other," were his precise words.

Despite all that, Ashlyn felt restless. She had to help her baby sister. She couldn't sit around and do nothing. That would eat her alive.

That was why she got so focused on Mason and his behavior, because she was devastated about her sister. It was somehow transferred since her marriage was already on rocky ground. Ashlyn was pretty obsessed with learning her husband's secrets.

She was filled with so much doubt and resentment that it made her take actions she would never dream of taking in the past.

She couldn't remain passive. That man was clearly keeping something from her. Something had changed that affected his mood and behavior toward her, and considering all that was happening around her, Ashlyn was highly motivated to find out what.

Although she had more pressing issues, and it would be more prudent to go home and spend time with her parents, like a woman possessed, she waited for Mason to go to work so she could snoop around his office.

Once she heard his car driving away, Ashlyn descended from her room and started to look about without wasting any time, although she knew he wouldn't return until evening.

The first thing she inspected was his massive desk. She rummaged through all kinds of papers, contracts, sketches, and other boring stuff.

Ashlyn didn't know what she was looking for. It wasn't like he would be keeping some other woman's mementos around. *Or would he?* So, she went through everything. She was like an IRS agent, fine-combing his personal space, looking for anything out of order. Looking for his secrets.

Ashlyn needed to know what he was up to. Because she was sure that since he wasn't spending any time with her, he must be spending it with someone else. That was just common sense.

Things between them were bad before the New Orleans trip, and now they were even worse. He'd completely pulled away again. Though he'd made promises, he'd not followed through on them and she couldn't help but think it was because he didn't really love her. He didn't really want to fix their marriage. And since their fight the other night, he'd not even spoken to her. He couldn't even be bothered to ask if there was any news regarding her sister.

He didn't care about anything other than himself. It was heartbreaking.

Wretchedly, that was not all. Even when they were not specifically fighting, just trying to share a meal, Ashlyn still caught herself wanting to fight. And that was not okay.

Mason was completely indifferent, and she was sure she would find proof why. That very morning, although they were both in the kitchen preparing breakfast, he hadn't asked whether there was any news regarding Karina or offered any kind of encouragement to remain strong as her family waited for the police to find her.

Perhaps it was wrong, but her pride didn't allow her to ask for his help again. He was a powerful man. He could learn everything the police weren't telling them if he asked, but something held her back from asking him to do that.

There was a big chance she would rot in hell, at least according to her mother's tales, for not doing everything in her power to help her sister, but considering how things stood between the spouses, she could not ask him to intervene. Deep down, she knew Mason was the kind of person who would hold something like that over her head in the future. She didn't want him to have that kind of power.

It saddened her to think of her husband in that way. That she was forced to look through his personal things. But it was a necessary evil.

He'd pushed her away, and she needed to know why no matter what. Even if it meant completely breaking her heart in the process. Realizing she'd stopped looking about as she contemplated everything, Ashlyn resumed her sneaky business.

At some point, she groaned in frustration. Everything in this damned room was work-related. Part of her wanted to say *well, duh,* and the rest kept looking about.

He spent a lot of time in this room, so it was logical to assume that if he wanted to keep something from her, it would be in there. Then again, if he were having an affair, would he keep evidence of his infidelity inside the house? She had a moment of doubt.

Regardless, she had to keep going. Perhaps he was arrogant enough to never dream she would ever suspect him of having an affair.

Ashlyn was searching through the last drawer when she found something unexpected. It looked like an old address book. No one used those these days, but Mason was old enough to have one.

She sifted through it, grasping for straws, when one name caught her attention.

In his handwriting, Mason had written Bella Adams, and underneath there was a home phone number.

She knew that name. Bella was Mason's mother. His estranged mother he never talked about. But he had her phone number.

On impulse, she tore the paper out of the address book, and folding it, placed it inside her pocket. She couldn't explain why, but it felt important to have that woman's contact information. Returning the address book as she found it, she closed the drawer. After making sure nothing on the desk looked overturned, she left the office.

On one hand, she'd found nothing about his affair. On the other, she still felt like she'd managed to accomplish something.

Thinking of Mason's mother, Ashlyn got a crazy idea. There was one problem, though: Ashlyn didn't know if she was brave enough, or desperate enough, to set things in motion.

I guess I will find out.

26

Ashlyn spent a lot of hours of the day staring at the piece of paper she'd torn from Mason's address book, staring at the contact info of his estranged mother as though that was the magical cure that could solve all her problems.

It wasn't.

Especially if she never gathered the courage to use it.

Each time she managed to convince herself to dial the number, speak with the woman, and finally learn what happened between Mason and his parents, she chickened out at the last moment.

This was one of those situations where she wanted to learn the truth, but didn't at the same time, because it could never be unlearned. What if there were something especially horrific?

You're acting like a baby, she snapped at herself, irritated at her cowardice.

If something terrible had happened, that was more reason to learn about it. Speaking with his parents would give her much-needed insight into Mason and what was currently happening with him.

Then again, she had been led to believe Mason's parents were a complete nightmare. No matter what was happening between her and her husband, the knowledge that they did him wrong still hung over her head. Calling his mother behind his back would be a major betrayal on her part.

He betrayed me first, she argued with herself. He was never around, and he was distant, at times even unnecessarily cruel. Considering all that, she had to do everything in her power to discover the truth.

She was full of questions and felt like this could provide her with a few answers. Of course, she didn't expect his parents to know whether he had a mistress, but they could show some insight. They'd known him longer than she had, after all.

Still, she hesitated. Maybe she could track Mason and find out for herself.

So one evening, after he'd pretty much ghosted her the entire night, she waited, listening for any sound of him leaving the house. She hadn't bothered getting ready for bed. Instead she'd stayed dressed and ready to go the moment she suspected him of leaving.

At ten after one, she heard the front door open. She hurried to the bedroom window and saw him getting into his car.

Quickly grabbing her keys, Ashlyn ran downstairs to the garage, got in her own car, and backed out, determined to follow him. He'd had enough of a head start that she knew he'd gotten out of the gate and was already well on his way to wherever he was going. If it was to his mistress's house, she'd catch him.

Ashlyn headed out of the gate and soon she could see his tail lights on the road ahead. She kept a good distance between them, and followed him as he drove around Tahoe. But that was all he did.

Had he figured out that she was following him?

Her guts twisted at the thought. He wasn't supposed to know that she was keeping an eye on him. And what if he went home and she wasn't there? Nerves had her making a right-hand turn and heading back home. It took an hour to get back there, and it was going on five a.m. by the time she pulled into the garage.

All she'd done was deprive herself of much-needed sleep, but it wasn't like she was sleeping much anyway with Karina missing. Still, she headed upstairs and went through her bedtime routine, even though it was nearly morning. She was tossing and turning when she heard his car pull up the drive. He couldn't have been more than thirty minutes behind her.

Despite the fact that there couldn't have been any time for him to visit a mistress, she was still sure he had one. She'd just have to find another way to discover her. Maybe she'd have to call his mom after all. It was her last resort.

She needed to do this for Karina as well. Ashlyn felt guilty that she was so preoccupied with her husband while her sister was missing. So, the sooner she dealt with this mess in her marriage, the better.

Later that morning, after she'd had a couple hours of sleep and she was sure that Mason had left for work, she found his mom's number and grabbed her phone. Taking a deep breath, Ashlyn dialed the number.

Then an eternity passed before someone answered and said, "Hello?"

The fairly young voice completely took her by surprise. *Does Mason have a younger sister?*

"Hello," Ashlyn recovered quickly. "May I speak with Mr. Adams or Mrs. Adams?" Ashlyn said politely.

Since she knew nothing about that household, knew nothing about their habits or what they did for a living, she figured it would be better if she covered her bases, and hoped at least one of Mason's parents was home.

There was a pause from the other side that confused her a little.

"Mr. Adams passed away three years ago."

Ashlyn made a face. She'd messed up that one. Of course, she'd had no idea he'd died. Did Mason? He never mentioned it. "Sorry to hear that. May I speak with Mrs. Adams then?"

"What should I say this is about? Who's calling?"

Ashlyn was not surprised that this person asked for details. She was a complete stranger, after all, and had made that perfectly clear.

"My name is Ashlyn Adams. Mrs. Adams is my mother-in-law," she explained. It felt strange to say that. She'd never met the woman, so although what she said was true, it still felt false.

"Please wait."

Wait she did. She also stressed a lot and bit her already too-short nails, since in her head she was already hearing a no from this woman, that Mrs. Adams didn't want to speak with her. There was a huge possibility that this woman didn't even know Mason was married.

"Hello?" a soft voice interrupted her thoughts.

"Hello, Mrs. Adams," Ashlyn said, not even trying to conceal how relieved she was to hear the other woman's voice. "My name is Ashlyn, and I'm... I'm your son's wife. Mason's wife," she added as though this woman might have forgotten her son's name.

She was acting like an idiot, and it couldn't be helped. She was stressed as hell.

"I know who you are, Ashlyn. I'm very aware my son got married, and honestly, I'm not surprised to receive this phone call, albeit a little later than expected."

"Excuse me?" she replied, frowning.

"I knew this day was coming," the other woman replied. It was obvious she planned on saying nothing else.

Ashlyn pressed forward. "I was wondering if you would be willing to meet with me. I would like to talk with you about your son." *To learn why he is the way he is.*

"Has something happened? Has he hurt you?"

Ashlyn was taken aback. "Hurt me?"

"Yes, has he hurt you?"

"No, never," she was quick to reassure. "Not physically anyway," she added.

"I see. But there are a number of ways he might have hurt you, my dear. Not all of them physical. Is that why you're calling?"

"Well, yes." Ashlyn was confused, but she couldn't deny that his mother was right and there were other ways of being hurt.

"I do not leave the house much these days, but you're more than welcome to come and visit."

Ashlyn nodded, although the other woman couldn't see her. "I would like that very much. When?"

"Tomorrow?"

"That would be perfect."

After she wrote down the address, raising an eyebrow in

discovering that Mrs. Adams was in the Tahoe area, and the instructions on how to find the estate, Ashlyn thanked her and disconnected.

For some reason, she felt like she could finally breathe again. This was a first step in the right direction. A step made toward learning about Mason, who he was, and what he was trying so hard to hide from her.

Was there a possibility that she was putting too much stock into this meeting? Definitely, but there wasn't much else she could do at that point, apart from confronting Mason.

He would just accuse her of being irrational, like he usually did, without actually engaging in a conversation.

Talking with his mother was her only option.

THE NEXT DAY, after Mason went to work, Ashlyn got into her car and started her journey.

Bella Adams lived about thirty minutes between Ashlyn's home and Tahoe. Ashlyn was sure that she would be able to return that evening before her husband, leaving him none the wiser. Because she was sure if he confronted her about her day, she would fumble. She had never been that good of a liar, so it was best not to come home later than he did.

Following precise instructions, and with Google Maps to guide her, Ashlyn had no problems finding the house.

It was hard not to gawk at the estate as she parked the car in the small parking lot next to the house. Mrs. Adams lived in a palace. That was the only way she could describe the monumental edifice in front of her.

Suddenly, she started to feel self-conscious and under-dressed, but she'd come this far so there was no going back.

Taking a deep breath, she exited the car and marched toward the front door.

A maid opened the door for her and showed her to a receiving room. That was what the maid had called it, not Ashlyn. Ashlyn didn't dare sit on such fine, delicate-looking furniture. She knew how expensive it was, being an interior designer and all.

After a couple of minutes, Bella Adams came to greet her.

She was nothing as Ashlyn had imagined. Mrs. Adams was in her sixties, slightly round, and soft-featured. She had graying brown hair that she didn't bother to dye, and her eyes were hazel. She was very well dressed, with a few choice pieces of jewelry that complemented her outfit.

Apart from the hair color, Ashlyn saw no resemblance between mother and son. Perhaps Mason looked like his father.

"Hello, Mrs. Adams. It's nice to finally meet you," Ashlyn said politely.

"You too, Mrs. Adams," the other woman said with a small smile.

"Oh, please, call me Ashlyn."

"Would you like some coffee or tea?" Mason's mother offered.

"Tea would be nice."

They moved to a closed garden where there was a small metal table set for two, and they settled. The maid brought the tea set, from which Mrs. Adams poured the steaming beverage into two cups.

Although Ashlyn was eager to dive into the conversation, some rules of etiquette had to be followed. They'd just met, after all.

"Do you mind telling me a bit about yourself?" Mrs. Adams requested.

And so, Ashlyn did. Without being asked, after finishing about personal stuff, she told how she'd first met Mason and how they came to be married.

Mrs. Adams nodded. "We heard he got married." She eyed her as she took a sip from her tea.

"Not what you expected?" Ashlyn blurted out before she could stop herself.

"Oh, no, dear. This is nothing against you. My late husband tried reaching out a few years back, but fell ill quite abruptly."

"I'm sorry for your loss. I didn't know."

"Thank you. We shared a lovely life." As she said that, a shadow passed over her face. It was obvious that part about a lovely life was only meant for her husband, not her son.

"Mrs. Adams, if you don't mind my asking, what happened between you and your husband and Mason?"

"And if I mind, would you leave?" the other woman said with a smile.

Ashlyn was completely confused.

"I was joking, my dear. I don't mind speaking about it. But I do have a question in return. What did he tell you about us?"

"Nothing much," she replied honestly. "He told me that the last time he saw you was right before he started college. He also mentioned that you abandoned him."

"I see." She paused there as though collecting her thoughts. "Well, the situation was slightly more complicated, as you can imagine."

"I figured."

"You being here must mean you've started to notice things about him."

Ashlyn nodded wholeheartedly, relieved she was finally with someone who would understand. "He's changed, and I don't know what to make of it."

"I'm not sure I understand what you mean by saying he's changed, dear. Mason has always been very…" She paused as though looking for the right words. "Uptight. Rigid. Uncompromising." She sighed. "There are many words I would use to describe my son, none of them complimentary, I'm afraid."

"I'm not sure I understand, now. That's not the Mason I know."

"Very well then, describe my son to me from your perspective."

Ashlyn thought about it and then said, "Well, when we first met and for the first four and a half years of our lives together, Mason was loving and kind and caring. We rarely fought. We made big plans for the future, starting a family and everything. He spent most of the last year building us our dream house so we could make that happen." She frowned and met Mrs. Adams' gaze. "But ever since we moved, he's been dismissive, distracted, uncaring… My sister has gone missing and it's like he couldn't care less how upset I am about it."

Mrs. Adams lifted her tea cup and sipped, then placed it back in her saucer. "My son is complicated. He's got a very unrealistic view of people and a controlling personality. He's definitely a narcissist."

Ashlyn could see the part about him being controlling but the rest she didn't understand. "What do you mean?"

Giving her a kind smile, Mrs. Adams said, "Did Mason tell you about his sister?"

"Sister?" Ashlyn was taken aback. Mason had always claimed he was an only child, and she said as much.

"I can imagine that he would prefer that to be the case. You see, his sister is, for lack of a better word, a mess. I love her to pieces, but for much of her former years, if there was a bad decision to be made, Madeline made it. And as controlling and narcissistic as Mason is, Madeline is his complete opposite. A free spirit, if you will. She ran off at fifteen, falling for a young man with a motorcycle and a bad reputation. He got her hooked on drugs, and had her doing things no proper young lady should be doing, if you take my meaning."

Ashlyn gasped. "What happened to her?" She didn't think from Mrs. Adams' words that she'd died, though she feared that might be the case.

"We were able to get her home and sent her to a detox facility, but Mason never forgave her for abandoning him. Those were his words. She'd abandoned him. He grew more rigid, more focused on himself. He pushed us all away. College didn't soften him. He just grew more distant from us, harsher in his views of his sister. Of us, for forgiving her and helping her. The last thing he ever said to Madeline was that she was a useless, worthless sister and he wished she'd died."

Ashlyn was shocked.

"So it doesn't surprise me at all that he's told you he was an only child. That he's using words to hurt you. That his behavior is hurting you." She sighed. "I don't know where we went wrong with him and I'm sorry, for what it's worth."

He'd lied to her. All this time, he'd been lying to her,

Ashlyn thought. What else was he lying about? Did he actually have a mistress? Had he used their arguments to deflect from the fact he no longer cared about her? Would he cut her out of his life as he'd done with his sister? With his parents?

Ashlyn didn't know what to do now. She was troubled on all fronts. Not only was her marriage on the rocks, but also her sister was missing. Her sister, who sounded a whole lot like Mason's own sister. Was that why he was always so antagonistic toward Karina? Could he have done something to her?

Ashlyn was frightened by that thought. Why would that even enter her mind? Mason wasn't a predator. A narcissist, yes, but a predator? One who kidnapped women? No. Besides, Karina wasn't the only woman missing. There were others. What reason would Mason have for kidnapping them? That didn't make sense.

"My dear, is something else troubling you?" Mrs. Adams reached across the table and patted her hand.

"Did Mason... has he ever physically hurt his sister?"

"Oh, no. Nothing beyond the usual siblings fights they had when they were children. Mason was always more cutting with his words than his fists, thankfully."

That at least was a relief to Ashlyn. She'd never not felt safe around Mason, so she felt it was good to be reassured that she hadn't missed that. "How is Madeline now?" she asked.

"She's doing well for the most part. She still struggles with some things, but she's met a lovely young man, and they live in Los Angeles. I go to see them often."

"That's good to hear," Ashlyn replied. She drank the last

of her tea. "Well, I should probably go. It was good to meet you," she said, standing.

"And you as well, dear. You're a sweet girl and I hope... well, I will just say I wish you well."

Ashlyn understood. "Thank you," she replied as she walked to the door. Turning back, she said, "If you'd like, I can try and get Mason to come and see you."

Mrs. Adams shook her head. "No. I'm afraid his knowing you came to see me at all will just cause more fighting between you, my dear. I came to terms with his disowning us long ago. Don't put your marriage into trouble just for me. I'll be fine."

Giving her a nod, Ashlyn left. What Mrs. Adams had shared made her sad for her husband, but her fears of him having a mistress weren't dismissed. If anything, she was even more determined to find who it was that he was seeing. And to find out if he had anything to do with Karina going missing as well.

That night, after returning home to prepare dinner, she received a text from Mason, telling her he wouldn't be home again. He claimed he had more meetings early in the morning, but Ashlyn didn't believe him. She was sure he was going to be with his mistress. She just didn't know what to do about it.

She didn't bother to text him back. Instead, she made herself dinner and then, after a hot bath, went to bed. She hoped for a good night's sleep, but found her dreams were anything but peaceful.

She couldn't recall much, but in them, the once-faceless man who'd been stalking her now wore Mason's face. Was it rational? No. It didn't matter though. Ashlyn's mind was a mess. She couldn't dismiss the idea that Mason was behind Karina's kidnapping.

No, that can't be right, she rebelled. She was stressed, sleep-deprived, and scared, not to mention angry at her husband, and that was the only reason something so horrific came to mind, she rationalized. Karina's kidnapping had nothing to do with Mason. This was some deranged man acting out on his impulses.

Besides, he doesn't own a van. She would have noticed it parked in the backyard.

Still, the thoughts wouldn't leave her head, so she decided to call his mother.

"Well, good morning, my dear. Is everything well with you?" Mrs. Adams greeted her.

"Yes. Well, no. Not really. Mrs. Adams, do you believe Mason is capable of kidnapping?" she asked.

"Why would you ask something like that?" the other women wondered, sounding surprised.

"There have been several kidnappings in the Tahoe area, all young women. Among them is my sister," Ashlyn explained.

"I'm so sorry to hear that, but why would you believe Mason has something to do with it?"

"I don't, but... well, my sister reminds me a lot of his sister and he's been so... distant lately. I don't know what to think."

"We lost touch a long time ago, and I suppose it's possible that he could be behind this, but I couldn't say for certain. What I can tell you is that when his sister started doing what she was doing, Mason was beside himself. He threatened to put an end to her behavior at the time, but he never went into detail as to what he meant by that. We got her home and into a drug rehab facility before he acted. At least, as far as I know that is the case." Mrs. Adams paused for a moment. "I know Mason never forgave us for it."

Ashlyn focused on the fact that Mason had said he wanted to put an end to his sister's behavior. Did that mean he wanted to kill her? Surely not, right? She was still his sister. He wouldn't do that, would he? Something akin to fear filled her. Mason didn't have a connection to Karina. Would he kill her?

"Okay, thank you. I just had to ask. I'm really worried about my sister, and I had this dream that Mason might be behind her kidnapping."

"I understand. Dreams can sometimes lead us to the truth, so I would just be careful in your interactions with my son, my dear. I remember Mason as a ruthless boy who doesn't forgive what he perceives as slights. And you accusing him of this would definitely be a slight."

"I will be careful. Though if he is behind my sister's disappearance, I plan to expose him," she promised.

If Mason had her sister and the police were useless to make the connection, then it was all on her to do the right thing, find Karina, and expose Mason.

"And in the meantime, if it is Mason behind all of this, may God help us all."

27

Ashlyn's head spun from everything she'd learned from Mrs. Adams and from her disturbing dreams. Her whole world was being destroyed by the simple notion that there was a possibility she was sleeping next to the serial kidnapper the authorities were looking for.

She said "possibility" because she had no proof, but Mason had stayed in the city, or at least told her that's where he was around the times several of those women went missing, maybe even all of them. And he had said they'd all been asking for trouble, so what if he was just making excuses for his actions? She didn't know for sure, but she thought it might definitely be possible. Which was why she was highly motivated to find out for Karina's sake.

After spending a little more time talking with Mrs. Adams on the phone, Ashlyn had said goodbye and started cleaning the house as she thought over everything she knew so far about the kidnapping victims, Mason and her sister.

She still had trouble accepting everything she'd learned

about Mason from his mother. It was so different from the man she'd fallen in love with. The man she'd married and been with for a little more than five years now. Had he simply been wearing a mask this whole time? Hidden his real personality? Or had she just not seen it? Not wanted to see it? She couldn't say, but she no longer trusted him, and that was a problem.

As she drove to Tahoe to see her parents, she wished her biggest problem was Mason's infidelity. But the thought that he could be behind her sister's disappearance, behind the other women's disappearances, had her thrown for a loop. Having women stashed someplace, to do God only knew what with them... She was too weakhearted to even contemplate something like that, and all the possibilities were beyond horrific.

Everything inside her urged her to leave him and never return, but she couldn't do that. Ashlyn couldn't leave him, not when he might be behind it all and Karina's life was at stake. Not to mention all the other women taken.

Ashlyn spent a while with her folks, trying to keep her mother busy and her father calm, but it was pretty useless. They were both terrified for Karina and there wasn't anything Ashlyn could do to fix that except for finding her sister. She wasn't sure how to go about that either. She wondered if Mason might have left some kind of clues in his sanctuary as to where—if he was the one behind everything —her sister was.

When she returned home, she looked toward his man cave. *Why am I not allowed inside it?*

Mason had never specifically forbidden her from going down to his private sanctuary, but over time it was somehow implied that it was his space alone. Why was he so adamant about that? Was he hiding something down there? There must be something he didn't want her to see.

She was pretty sure none of the women were inside the house. She would have heard someone calling for help if they were, but all the same, Ashlyn became convinced she would uncover at least some of his secrets going down there.

Unfortunately, that would have to wait for tomorrow, because she ran out of time. She could hear his car approaching, and saw the taillights flashing as he parked.

Ashlyn had no time to collect her thoughts or put on a poker face before Mason entered the house a few minutes later.

That was close, she thought as her heart started to race like crazy. If she'd attempted to go downstairs, he would have caught her in the act. She couldn't let him catch her.

She moved from the hall to sit in the living room. Her hands started to shake. She was not ready to see him. She couldn't bear it, not after learning he'd lied to her and was possibly behind all of this.

Pull yourself together, she snapped.

Mason couldn't know something was wrong. Everything depended on his oblivion. Everything depended on her, so she needed to be strong, now more than ever.

She had just turned on the TV as he walked through the front door. It was obvious he was not in the best of moods. That made her even more nervous.

"Where have you been?" he demanded, looking at her with a deep frown on his face.

That startled her. "I was with my parents, trying to comfort them," she said, stumbling a little. She hoped her nervousness would be interpreted as stress caused by her sister's kidnapping.

Did you do it, Mason?

"You shouldn't be all alone on the road at night," he berated.

"They needed me."

"Of course." It took him a moment to calm down and then he asked, "Still no word?"

"No."

Was he relieved that was the case? She tried to see clues on his face, and there was nothing. Was it possible that he was that good an actor?

"Have you eaten?"

"Yes," she lied again.

"Good." He went in for a kiss, and Ashlyn barely stopped herself from flinching.

Her whole life was a lie. The man she'd fallen in love with had lied to her for their entire relationship.

She stopped herself because that line of thinking was bound to send her spiraling, and she had to remain calm and focused to be able to do what was right. And of course, there was a small chance she was blowing it all out of proportion and Mason was completely innocent. At least of the kidnappings. The problem was that it wasn't looking that way to her.

To her surprise, after kissing her, he sat down on the sofa next to her.

"It has been a long day. I've missed you," he said, taking her into his arms.

Ashlyn closed her eyes. *Get a grip on yourself. Breathe.* She'd always loved Mason's arms being around her. She needed to focus on that. "I know the feeling," she managed to choke out.

"Is everything all right?"

Crap. "No," she replied honestly. "I don't know how long my parents will be able to go through this."

"Everything will be all right, my love." Although he said all the right things at the right time, for the first time, she noticed something else. He was only placating her. He seemed almost irked that he was forced to speak about her sister.

"You will always have me," he added unexpectedly, tightening his grip ever so slightly.

The way he said it was odd to Ashlyn. As though he thought she might doubt him. Did he know that she was? Swallowing hard, she gave him a tentative smile. "I know," she replied because she sensed that was what he expected.

And then he kissed her again. Ashlyn went with it. And then he continued to kiss her.

Once upon a time, she would interpret this as his way of trying to comfort her, yet now all she saw were deceit and selfishness. Was he trying to make up for the fact he had no real empathy for her sister being missing? Was it that he didn't really care about her but felt guilty for having a mistress? Or was it something else? Something more sinister?

She was disgusted by her thoughts and by his behavior. It was more sinister, and she had to put in an effort not to stop him, move away from him, or run away from him as far as possible.

To her utmost horror, he deepened the kiss, and Ashlyn instantly knew where this was going. She knew all his moves by then. They'd been married for five years, after all.

Sure enough, he stood up and took her to the bedroom. While they climbed the steps, all she thought about was whom he might have been with last. Was it her? Or was it some other woman? His mistress? Or worse... one of the kidnapped women? Her sister? That thought disgusted her.

And no amount of *don't think about it* helped.

She dreaded being with him right now. She couldn't stand the way her thoughts were leading her to believe that he was somehow behind the kidnappings. The idea of it was making her sick to her stomach.

"Let me make you feel better," he breathed against her skin as he slowly took her clothes off.

She went with it, naturally.

You can do this, she encouraged, forcing herself to kiss him back.

Sure, she could have said she wasn't in the mood and rejected his advances, but she was doing her best to avoid any confrontations or arguments. She feared if she said no, Mason would lash out and demand an explanation. One she wasn't prepared to give until she could discover the answers she was after. She feared the worst, but she wasn't about to accuse him without proof. If he was guilty, he might do to her what he'd done to the others. If he was innocent... then he'd never forgive her. His mother had said as much.

He had never been violent with her, except that one time during sex. There was no telling if that could change. Or what he would do to someone else, if it was true that the kidnapped women were taken by him. So that was a risk she wasn't willing to take.

Ashlyn was full-on terrified of this situation. If he was behind all of this, if he was guilty of all the heinous things her mind conjured, and then kissing her, impersonating a loving husband but really being some criminal mastermind with who knew what intent, what did that make her? Despite that, she did the only thing she could to make this moment bearable. She thought of the bigger picture. This was one small act for the greater good.

Keeping Mason happy meant she'd have another chance to investigate whether he was guilty or not. Whether he had a mistress or not. Whether she should leave him or not.

Ashlyn went through the motions, completely disconnected emotionally, doing all she was supposed to on autopilot, pretending all was well, pretending she wanted him when in reality, her mind was running through worst-case scenarios. Her whole world could come crashing down, and there was nothing she could do to stop it.

Ashlyn did her best to observe him and the way he behaved, the way he spoke. The more she looked, the more she noticed there were small fractures in his actions, in his words, in the looks he gave her. They seemed forced somehow. Like he was merely an actor playing a part on the stage.

How could she have been so blind?

There seemed to be traces of cruelty in him, in his eyes, in his smirk, the way he phrased certain things. She couldn't believe this was the man she'd married. How could she have been so blind? Karina had been right about him all along.

Is that the reason he kidnapped her? she wondered. Not that it mattered. The only thing that mattered was getting her back. And for that to happen, she would do whatever it took, even sleep with him. She would deceive him just like he'd been deceiving her. That was only fair.

He'd lied to her for five years, pretending he had loved her, when he was a lying cheat and a bastard who might have kidnapped multiple other women. *Why did he notice me? Why did he marry me?*

Was there something about her that made him think she was like him? Cruel and callous? He'd obviously thought she would drop her family the moment he suggested it. Had he done that because that was what he would do? Ashlyn began to wonder if Karina being missing was her own fault. Had Mason resorted to kidnapping to get her out of their lives? Ashlyn wanted to scream at the thought.

Those were the thoughts passing through her head as he made love to her. He still told her all the same things, he still touched her the way she loved, and she had to fight back tears since this was all breaking her heart. Her whole marriage was nothing but a lie. Everything he ever said and did was a lie.

Did he ever love me, one bit? She didn't dare answer that question because a mental breakdown was the last thing she needed at the moment. She couldn't allow herself to fall apart. Afterward, when all was accomplished and she knew the truth for sure, she could allow herself to lose control, cry her eyes out, and mourn all that was lost, if her fears were proven true. Yet not before.

"You're the only one in this world for me, my love," he said to her afterward, holding her in his arms, moving his long fingers through her hair, lulling her to sleep.

Ashlyn pretended to doze off. She had other plans tonight. Besides, she'd slept through too much already. Or so it felt, as though the last five years of marriage she had been asleep and was now finally waking up to reality, to the real man beside her, not the fantasy version she'd married.

Later that night, just as she predicted, Mason sneaked out of bed, and she went after him. She counted seconds inside her head, giving him some lead before following him.

He disappeared into his man cave, like she suspected he would, and once again she gave him some time before trying the handle to go downstairs as well.

The door was locked. She fumed.

What was she supposed to do now? Taking any kind of tool to the door was out of the question because Mason would definitely hear that.

After a couple of minutes of standing there like an ornament, staring at the door handle as though it would magically open, she decided to give up.

Tomorrow, when he goes to work, I'm getting in there, she told herself.

She just hoped her sister had that much time. She dismissed that thought, returning to bed.

Ashlyn couldn't sleep at all that night, waiting to see when or if Mason would return. Close to dawn, he did and even fell asleep for a few hours, before waking up acting well-rested once the alarm clock went off.

I missed so much, she thought glumly, watching him getting ready for another day. But she definitely saw a difference now. He was different. And she couldn't unsee it.

Even if he was innocent, Ashlyn didn't know if things would ever be the same again.

How could they?

28

Ashlyn planned to snoop around Mason's man cave first thing in the morning, but Mason decided to linger and spend the morning working from his office. Which wasn't that strange, yet at the same time, it was highly suspicious.

She was scared to be alone with a man who pretended to be her loving husband, and she was concerned it would show, especially since she was sleep-deprived and on her last nerve. So she muttered how she needed to see her parents and left the house in haste before he had a chance to say anything in return.

On her way to her parents' house, Ashlyn tried her best to collect her thoughts. To be perfectly honest, she'd been trying to do so from the moment Karina went missing, to no success.

Having to talk with her parents and share with them all she'd learned would probably be the hardest thing she would have to do in her entire life.

She didn't even know where to begin. *How do you tell*

someone you love that you're responsible for their misery? Because she was. She'd brought Mason into their lives, and these were the direct consequences of that. They may lose a daughter.

Don't you dare think like that.

It was extremely difficult wondering what Mason was doing inside his man cave, wondering if he'd truly kidnapped all those women, her sister.

Should I just call the police? She'd asked herself that same question many times over the last several days. To most people, it would be the most logical thing to do, yet Ashlyn was on the precipice. Because what if she was wrong? What if they found nothing? What if Mason was innocent?

What if all of this was nothing more than a figment of her worried mind? What if she managed to convince herself of a certain narrative to be able to deal with the guilt that she hadn't been there to prevent Karina from leaving the house that night?

Yet there was another concern. What if Mason was involved, but because of his wealth and power, he got tipped off on what was going on? What if the police stormed the house only to discover nothing? It would be disastrous if he was the kidnapper, because in a panic, there was no telling what he would do to those poor women.

That was why she decided to stay silent for a bit and see if she could discover some proof first on her own.

Ashlyn couldn't stop thinking about all the women taken. She had to find them, no matter what. The main question was, where was he keeping them? And she was sure she could find answers in the basement.

However, that was not the only thing running through her head.

What did he do with them? Assuming he was the one who took them. Albeit that question might be the obvious one, it froze the blood inside her veins. *Those poor souls.* She prayed for them to be strong.

What plagued her the most was whether they were still alive; whether Karina was alive. It didn't matter that they'd never found a body. They were surrounded by so many acres of forest it wouldn't be hard for someone to dispose of a body if they wanted to.

No, they are alive. She forced herself to stop traveling down that dark path. She couldn't fathom why that monster was taking women, but she had to have faith that she would find them, all alive. She had to keep that faith because if she lost that, then it was all for nothing.

Her mother noticed something was wrong with her as soon as she arrived. Although she decided to tell them everything during her stay, she felt conflicted and chickened out a couple of times.

However, once she started to feel too overwhelmed, too guilty for keeping something so monumental from them, Ashlyn turned off the TV, wanting to make sure she had her parents' full attention, especially her father's, before she started to speak.

Her mother looked at her with concern. "Is something the matter?"

In the midst of all of this, her heartbreak over Karina, her mother was obviously still equally worried about Ashlyn.

Reminding herself once again that her parents deserved to hear the truth, she nodded. After all, their daughter was missing, and it was all Ashlyn's fault.

"Do you know something?" her mother said.

Her father added, "Is Karina seeing that Paul character

again? Is she with him?" Although he appeared mad, it was obvious, in his eyes, that he preferred that scenario over the existing one.

Me too.

Ashlyn wasn't surprised his mind went that way. Paul and Karina had shared a very difficult, turbulent history. Their whole relationship was completely toxic, not to mention some of the things Paul did were illegal, so he was constantly putting Karina at risk.

"No, she wasn't seeing Paul." To her knowledge, that was. "But there is something I think you should know."

This time, her parents didn't interrupt her and looked at her expectantly, waiting to hear her discovery.

Here we go. "I think Mason has something to do with the kidnappings."

Her father stared at her incredulous. "What?"

"Look, he never liked Karina, and he's been erratic and irrational of late. And he's got weird, controlling behaviors—not to mention sneaking out in the middle of the night—and I think it could be him," she rambled, looking everywhere else apart from at her parents. As she spoke, she started to doubt herself.

"What are you talking about, Ashlyn? You're making no sense," her mother cried out, clearly rattled.

"How is Mason involved?"

Taking a deep breath, she tried again. "Mason leaves the house a lot at night. He was in Tahoe the night Karina went missing. He vanishes a lot, and I don't know where he is or what he's doing," she said, massaging her brow. She wasn't making much sense as she tried to explain how she'd come to the conclusion that Mason was involved in not only Karina's kidnapping but all the others as well.

"Why do you think he kidnapped Karina?" her mother asked.

"I'm not sure about anything. I just think it's possible he's the kidnapper," she insisted. "I feel like I'm losing my mind." That was God's honest truth. She had all these contradictory thoughts and didn't know what was true or false anymore.

"Maybe he's fooling around," her father offered.

"No." Ashlyn was adamant, even though she'd thought the same herself, still thought it was possible if she was honest, but she didn't want to tell her dad that, for some irrational reason.

"What did he do?" her father demanded.

"Nothing. Everything... I don't know." Ashlyn sighed. "I started noticing changes in him, and as I said, he's rarely home, and when he is home, he locks himself in the basement."

Her mother and father shared a look. It was obvious they were communicating something as only married people could.

Ashlyn bit her lip and pushed on. "So I went and visited his mother."

That made them both look at her. Like Ashlyn, her parents knew nothing about Mason's parents, or more accurately put, they knew what she'd told them, how they were estranged and didn't communicate.

"I got into contact with her and went for a visit. I learned his father passed away three years ago."

"Why did you want to see her?" her mother asked, confused.

Ashlyn shrugged. "I don't know. I was so confused. I wanted to speak with someone who knew him."

"And what did she say?" her father interjected.

All the worst things imaginable. "Basically, that he's a narcissist. He's ruthless, and controlling, and unforgiving."

"Okay... How does that make him a kidnapper?" her father questioned.

"It doesn't but there's more." Ashlyn then proceeded to explain to her parents everything she'd learned from Mrs. Adams about Mason having a sister and what happened with her. How Mason cut her and his parents off. How he had disowned them. How he had wanted to do something about his sister and the boy she'd run off with, but hadn't been able to, and how Mrs. Adams made it sound like he might have done something to them had he gotten his hands on them.

To say her parents were shocked would be an understatement. Her mother held her cross, which she wore around her neck, the entire time.

"Well, that is certainly something to be concerned about," her mother said.

"I always knew something was off with him," her father practically spat.

It was obvious he had half a mind to go and confront him that very moment, and Ashlyn prayed it wouldn't come to that.

"So you see why I think he might have done it?" she questioned.

"If he did, he's going to regret it," her father replied, looking pissed off.

"We need proof that he's involved, though," she pointed out the obvious.

"Leave that to the police. Stay here with us. Don't go home," her mother said as her father agreed with a nod.

"I can't do that," Ashlyn countered, much to her parents' chagrin.

"Why not? You just said you suspect him to be a kidnapper. How can you go back to such a man?"

"Your mother is right. Stay here, and I'll deal with that creep."

"You will do no such thing. I will go back and find something useful."

"Ashlyn, you're making no sense," her mother argued.

Ashlyn took a deep, stabilizing breath before replying, "It has to be me, Mom, because he doesn't suspect me. And if he has Karina and all the rest, then we can't allow the police to barge inside. What if he hurts them?"

Her mom put a hand over her mouth as though trying to stifle a cry.

On the other side of the small couch, her father still looked ready to kill, clenching and unclenching his fists.

Although he had never been violent with them, Ashlyn knew her father had been a brawler in his youth. Besides, what parent wouldn't hurt a person hurting their child?

"I still think we should tell the police everything and let them deal with it," her mother said.

"And what if I'm wrong? Or worse, what if I'm right?" Ashlyn countered.

"I don't understand."

"What if I'm right and we tipped him off with our behavior? No, Mason cannot suspect that we think he's the one kidnapping these women," Ashlyn insisted. "I don't want him hurting Karina because of me. So far, none of the women taken have ended up dead. Let's keep it that way." She knew she had to be blunt so they could see hers was the only way.

"I'm scared, Ashlyn. Scared for Karina, but I'm scared for you too."

"I know, Mom. Just trust me. I know what I'm doing," she said with a lot more confidence than she had.

In reality, she had no idea what she was doing since there was a big chance that she'd completely lost her mind. All the same, she felt in her entire being that this was the right course of action. It had to be him. Right? It was the only thing that made sense. Except there was a little niggle of doubt lurking in the back of her mind. What if she was wrong? What if she was about to blow up her marriage for nothing?

Ashlyn shook her head. No. She had to be right. Everything pointed to Mason. His irrational behavior, the way he was so callous about the kidnapped women, his hatred of Karina... how he wasn't home at the times the women were taken... it all fit.

Her father leaned forward. "So, what do you plan on doing, exactly?"

"I will get to the bottom of things. While he's at work, I'll search for evidence of his involvement."

"What if you find something?"

"I'll come straight here, and together, we will go to the police," she reassured.

Her mom shook her head. "I still don't like it. It's too dangerous."

"I'll pack an emergency bag and make sure I leave before he suspects anything."

"Promise?" her mother insisted.

"I promise, Mom."

"I want to come with you," her dad said.

"No, that's a bad idea and would make Mason suspicious," she pointed out.

Besides, imagining her father confronting Mason was just too horrific and sent shivers down her spine. She wouldn't allow Mason to hurt another member of her family.

"Call us all the time," her mom stressed.

"I will," she promised in return.

"If I don't hear back from you, I'm coming to the house," her father said grudgingly.

"Everything will be all right," Ashlyn replied, hoping like hell that she was telling the truth.

29

No matter how much Ashlyn tried, she could not keep her eyes open. Her plan was to follow Mason tonight, considering she couldn't bust into his man cave while he was in the house, yet after drinking her tea and going upstairs to get away from Mason and his shrewd eyes, she suddenly felt bone tired.

It was no wonder she was so suddenly overcome with fatigue considering she'd barely slept after someone had kidnapped Karina, so she saw no other way than to change her plans, leave everything for tomorrow, and go to sleep.

She hoped Mason would leave the house first thing in the morning so she could pack a bag, then go to his man cave and give it a thorough search in hopes she would find clues to where her sister and all the other women were.

That was the only place she hadn't searched, so if he had something to hide—and she believed he did—then it would be down there.

She barely touched the pillow before she lost consciousness. It didn't take long for the nightmares to start.

The maniac was inside the house again. Ashlyn knew that with every part of her being, although she couldn't see him yet. She was sure that the monster lurked in the shadows waiting for the right opportunity to attack, which was why it was so imperative for Ashlyn to reach the front door and escape. For some reason, she couldn't. No matter how much she tried, no matter how much effort she put into it, she couldn't lift her legs from the bed. They felt too heavy.

Come on, come on, *she urged. She knew she was running out of time yet was additionally in a panic about what was happening to her. Did that monster already do something to her without her realizing it?* Am I paralyzed? *she thought, wanting to hit her legs. Sadly, she couldn't move her arms either.*

What is happening to me? *She was fully conscious—at least she thought she was. She knew she was inside her bedroom, lying on her bed, but that was all she could feel. Her body refused to listen to her commands.*

No, no, no, no. *This couldn't be happening.* Not now. *She had to get away.*

When nothing worked, she even started to pray. Please, please, God. I don't want to die here.

Although she couldn't see anyone around her, the house didn't feel empty. And while she tried to force her useless body to start working again, she heard it. A small sound at first, but it grew. The maniac was reaching for her.

Ashlyn doubled her efforts, not that it did her any good.

She needed to leave that bed, leave the house, yet what she wanted didn't matter.

No, *she cried out stubbornly, frantically looking about. The bedroom door was open, and although only darkness poured inside from the hallway, she knew that such deep darkness couldn't be fully natural.*

Please, please, *she continued to pray, not even sure to whom.*

Maybe if she closed her eyes, it would turn out that this was nothing, only a bad dream, she thought out of pure desperation, doing just that.

Come on, Ashlyn, wake up, wake up, *she begged in her mind.*

Unfortunately, having her eyes closed made everything even worse. All the sounds were heightened. Was there someone crying?

That made her open her eyes again. Looking immediately toward the door, she was startled to see Karina next to her bed.

Where did she come from? Not that it mattered at the moment. Her wrists were completely bloody, she noted with horror. The maniac had hurt her. That crazy maniac had hurt her sister.

"Karina, what happened to you?" *she asked and wasn't sure what came out. Her mouth felt kind of strange.*

"Come on, Ash, wake up. I need you," *her sister urged, and as she spoke, she looked behind herself, as though in fear.*

That made Ashlyn frown since her words made no sense. Was Karina on drugs? She was perfectly awake, wasn't she? But Ashlyn couldn't move. There was something wrong with her.

"Karina, I can't move." *She tried again, yet it was as though her sister couldn't hear her.* "Karina, I'm stuck. I'm trying to find you, Karina, I swear."

"Come on, Ash. Please, I need you to find me," *her sister begged.*

Ashlyn had never seen her sister looking like that, so afraid.

All of a sudden, a dark figure approached.

Ashlyn started to panic, but she still couldn't move no matter how hard she tried. "Look out," *she tried to warn Karina.*

Her sister started to turn, but unfortunately, it was too late.

The figure grabbed her from behind in a tight embrace. As she was prepared to scream, a hand was placed over her mouth, and she was dragged away as she struggled.

It all happened so fast, but Ashlyn heard her sister pleading for help, despite being restrained. Begging Ashlyn to help her, to come find her before it was too late.

"No," Ashlyn screamed. "Leave her alone."

Why wouldn't her useless body move? She had to help her sister. She had to save her.

Karina's screams grew fainter with each passing second. She had lost her, and there was nothing she could do about it. And then the darkness clouded her vision and Ashlyn heard nothing else. Could see nothing else.

"No," Ashlyn sobbed. *This couldn't be happening.*

Her mind drifted in the darkness, and she felt the menacing presence again, but she was no longer in her bed. Now she was in her car, driving down the dark road between her home and Tahoe. Glancing in the rearview mirror, Ashlyn saw headlights, so bright they filled the mirror. Her heart rate sped up and she could feel herself starting to panic. The lights grew closer. So close she could see the grill of the van as though it was less than an inch behind her. The van was going to ram her!

Screaming, Ashlyn woke, jarring herself up in the bed. Her breath was labored as she tried to calm herself. "It was just a dream. It was just a dream," she repeated over and over again.

As she began to calm, she recalled the first part of the dream, when Karina had visited her, and she couldn't move at all. That had been weird. Why couldn't she move? Ashlyn raised her hand and sighed with relief when her arm and hand actually moved. And then she felt silly for believing she was actually paralyzed. Maybe she hadn't been able to move because she felt powerless in her life and didn't know how to help her sister, so in her dream she couldn't move a muscle.

And this is all happening because of Mason, isn't it? she thought.

It was then her mind drifted back to the dream, and she recalled the white van trying to ram her. She'd seen a van on the street outside her parents' house. And she'd seen it occasionally as she'd driven around Tahoe as well, usually when she'd had that feeling of being stalked. Had Mason been following her?

Ashlyn frowned. When would Mason have bought a van and why would he follow her? Was she wrong? Was there someone else doing all of this? Ashlyn needed to know the truth. To do that she had to go see what Mason was hiding in the basement.

She stood up, unable to remain in that bed, and not because of what she dreamed about. That was her bed that she shared with Mason, and the mere thought that he might be behind everything had her stomach roiling.

Is he really a monster? Is he behind all of this?

Banishing those useless thoughts, she got dressed. She hoped Mason had left by now so she could start snooping around. However, before she started to pack and search for evidence, she needed to make sure he was actually out of the house.

When she didn't move to do that, it had nothing to do with her muscles. She dreaded being in his presence. *Come on, you have to do it.*

She needed to do it. She couldn't lose her shit now. Karina needed her.

The key is in the basement. I have to check out the basement.

Ashlyn's mind drifted back to the dream. She had to find

Karina. And if somehow Mason was behind this and he had her sister locked in the basement, she was going to kill him. She had no idea how he'd have managed to do something like that, but it was the only thing that made sense. That was where he spent all his time.

Of course, wouldn't she have heard a bunch of women down there? She hesitated for a moment, but then recalled that Mason had already given her the answer as to why she might not have. He'd soundproofed the walls. She swallowed hard.

What if he's been keeping all of those women inside this house all this time? she thought with dread.

Oh, my God. Her heart raced like crazy.

The answer had been in front of her all along, and she wanted to smack herself on the head for being so blind.

They're in the basement. They have to be! That was why he was down there so much. Not to play video games, but to assault those women!

Now she was definitely sick to her stomach. Luckily, being so early in the morning, she had nothing to throw up.

Pull yourself together, she snapped at herself.

She couldn't continue to waste time up there, sniveling and acting like a coward. A lot depended on her, and she wasn't going to fail. She would find Karina and all the other women, and she would make sure Mason got exactly what he deserved.

30

Ashlyn tentatively went downstairs. She felt tense, expecting Mason to jump out in front of her, yet luckily, he didn't.

He'd gone to work already. She was sure of that. Not only by going into his office, but seeing his car was gone. She sighed with relief, although the knot inside her stomach remained. With him gone, it only meant it was time to go to the basement.

Shortly after reaching the door, she confronted her first obstacle. The door was locked again. She should have known. If he was hiding someone inside, no wonder he didn't want anyone going downstairs and snooping around.

Ashlyn, you were blind for too long. Not to mention extremely stupid. As she berated herself, she took the master key, the key her husband swore would be able to unlock all the doors, and it failed. It didn't fit the lock.

He'd lied. Then again, was she that surprised?

Ashlyn scoffed at the door. Unfortunately, the thing did not open from the intensity of her stare. This time around, she was not going to let this piece of wood stop her from her objectives.

She knew Mason had the key, and he probably carried it with him. At the same time, a control freak like him had to have a spare stashed somewhere as well. Without wasting time, Ashlyn rushed to his office to search for the spare key. Although it was still fairly early, Ashlyn was aware there was a ticking clock looming over her head and that she needed to be quick about all she did.

She looked in every drawer and came up empty-handed.

Where would Mason put it? It had to be somewhere easily accessible but hidden from her, she mused.

This is impossible, she thought in exasperation a few minutes later.

She was about to go and grab some power tools and demolish that door, bust inside, when her gaze landed on a cigar case on one of the shelves. That made her frown because she knew full well that Mason didn't smoke. He considered it a nasty habit, evidence of a weak individual who succumbed to a filthy addiction. And that was a direct quote.

Ashlyn grabbed the box, and opening it, found a bunch of cigars. And nothing else. Not giving up, she removed them and felt like crying when she spotted a key at the bottom.

Found you, she thought with elation.

Grabbing it, she felt triumphant, although this was no cause for celebration. She was trying to go to the basement to confirm her husband liked to kidnap women, after all.

Returning to the basement door, her relief was palpable as she tried the key and it actually fit. Taking a deep breath, she opened the door.

Let's see if my husband is a monster or not, she joked so she wouldn't cry.

Ashlyn started to descend the stairs, slowly, carefully, silently, and coming to the bottom, she saw only what she expected to see prior to all this mess and what he'd told her this place would be.

As far as she could gather, it was pretty much a typical man cave setup. It was somewhat different than when she'd first seen it, but still pretty much the same.

It was built to resemble a living room, with a big couch and an even bigger TV. As she'd seen when he showed her before, there was a PlayStation and a slew of vintage games. On the side wall there was a built-in bar, fully stocked, with a mirror on the wall behind the bottles.

Looking about, she found a small storeroom that held a ladder, a shelving unit with cleaning supplies, and there was even a toilet and sink. A second door led into the wine cellar. And that was it. There was nothing suspicious or out of the ordinary.

Then why was the door locked? It made no sense to her.

There has to be something else down here, she rebelled. Something she was missing.

Mason had built this whole house, designed everything on his own, so perhaps there were some hidden rooms, hidden parts of the house.

She looked everywhere in desperation, moving the carpet out of the way to see if there were hidden doors that led deeper into the ground.

Still, she discovered nothing.

Hidden doors would not be called hidden if they were so easily found.

What if there were false walls and secret passageways? In

any other circumstance, she would feel ridiculous thinking something like that but at the moment everything looked plausible to her.

Feeling like she had nothing to lose, Ashlyn started knocking against the walls, checking them, making sure they were real. If she was right, like her gut feeling was telling her, one, if not more, of them had to be false, hiding a door or something.

Come on, come on, I know you're here.

She proceeded with her task meticulously, making sure not to miss anything, but there was nothing there. No hidden doors, no false walls. Nothing.

Sinking down on the sofa, Ashlyn didn't see the remote control until she sat on it and the TV turned on. She gasped when she heard a woman crying out and looked up to see porn on the TV. Not just any kind of porn, it was BDSM porn. Ashlyn's jaw dropped. Mason liked this sort of thing? Was that why he'd kidnapped those women?

She frowned. If he had kidnapped them, then where were they? She'd found no sign of them here at the house. And if they weren't here, then where was he keeping them? Was she wrong? Was Mason innocent of the kidnappings?

She turned the TV off and stood up. Pacing the room, she thought about everything. Went back over the things she'd learned about the young women who'd gone missing. Had Mason been gone when they'd been taken? She couldn't be sure. And that white van the police said showed Karina being forced into it... Mason didn't own one as far as she knew. And wouldn't Karina or her parents have recognized Mason in the video?

But his animosity toward Karina... his non-empathy for the women taken... Ashlyn was so confused. She didn't know what to think. She didn't know if Mason was guilty or not. All she knew was she had to get away. She couldn't stay in this house until she had the answers to her questions. She needed to leave Mason. She just hoped she could get out of the house before he came home.

That decided, she rushed up the stairs and slammed the door to the basement behind her. The house was thankfully still quiet as she raced up the stairs to her bedroom and yanked a bag from the closet.

Hurrying, Ashlyn tossed as many clothes into her bag as possible. She wasn't even sure anything matched, and she didn't really care. Racing into the bathroom, she grabbed her toiletries and then zipped the bag closed. Within minutes she was downstairs, grabbing her car keys and heading toward the garage.

She had to get away. That was the only thing playing through her mind.

As she left the driveway, turning toward Tahoe, she noticed a white van on the side of the road in her rearview mirror. Was it Mason? Her heart began to race as she pressed on the gas.

Distance.

She needed distance. "Please, God, let me get away."

Her prayer went unanswered as she noticed the van pull onto the street and begin following her, their speed increasing as they rapidly approached.

31

Ashlyn's heart raced like crazy to the point that was the only thing she could hear. It made her hyperventilate as she drove down the quiet street at a rate of speed to envy an Indy race car driver. The van was right on her bumper and panic filled Ashlyn's chest.

The van's front rammed into the back of her sedan and caused the car to fishtail on the road. Ashlyn's knuckles were white as she held tight to the steering wheel, trying to keep the vehicle from going into the ditch. The van slammed into her again, this time at a slight angle, and she couldn't correct. The sedan went flying into the steep ditch on the right and as she impacted the embankment, her airbag deployed in her face.

Ashlyn blacked out.

When she came to, she cried out in pain and reached up to her hair as it was being pulled. It was then she realized she was being dragged by her hair out of the car. "Stop! Stop, you're hurting me!"

"Shut up, you fucking bitch!" It was a man's voice. Not

one she immediately recognized though. "Think you're so good. Too good for me, you snobbish whore. You're not."

Ashlyn couldn't understand what this man had against her. She'd never met him in her life as far as she was aware. "Who the fuck are you? Why are you doing this?" she cried out as her lower half hit the pavement.

He'd been dragging her on the grass at first, which wasn't so bad, but now she was getting road rash from her skin scraping on the asphalt. He yanked her hard, ignoring her question as he stopped next to the van. A moment later, his fist flew toward her face, and she blacked out again.

The movement of the van woke her. She cracked her eyes open. Her nose throbbed, and her head ached like never before. She struggled to see where she was, but the interior of the van was dark. There was no light at all. She opened her eyes more fully and tried to move, but found herself bound with her arms behind her back and her ankles tied together.

She couldn't understand what was going on. All she knew was that she'd been wrong about Mason. At least she was pretty sure now she'd been wrong. Maybe this guy had nothing to do with those other women going missing? Maybe Mason paid this guy to kidnap her?

Her mind was whirling with so many different scenarios. The biggest question she had was why was this happening to her?

The van came to a stop and shut off. She heard the driver get out and close the door. A moment later, the back doors opened, and he reached for her. As he dragged her out, she hit her head on the bumper, causing her to see stars.

He didn't speak, didn't say another word as he dragged her down a long corridor with cement floors. Single light bulbs hung from the ceiling, swinging slightly as they passed under each of them. It was creepy as fuck.

"Where have you taken me?" Ashlyn demanded.

"Be quiet. Things like you are not allowed to speak." He stopped and slammed his fist into her face, causing her to black out again.

She was in and out as he carried her, and not too gently, down a set of stairs.

I'm going to die down here, she thought.

Ashlyn tried to resist, tried to prevent that from happening. Sadly, it was all in vain. Her body was pretty beaten up, and the pain prevented her from controlling it. She was nothing but a lump of flesh in his arms, and each time she tried to speak, he hurt her even more.

Her heart sank as they reached a large cement room that made her think of a typical basement. No one was going to find her. Not here. How could they? Nobody knew where she was.

At least she was still alive, part of her pointed out.

For how long? But no matter the circumstances, she couldn't succumb to despair, although that was exactly what she wanted.

Her eyes had started to swell, but she forced herself to look about. Strangely, in the dim lighting, she noticed the walls were rounded in appearance. There were no corners in the room. That was very odd. Where on earth was she?

Rattling chains caught her attention, and she started to see movements and shapes. Her damn eyes weren't working properly anymore. However, her ears worked slightly better, and despite the ringing, she heard gasps as they entered. Was it the other kidnapped women? Were they here? Was Karina here?

And then one sound became more dominant than the others.

"What the fuck have you done to her?" a familiar voice demanded to know, cursing the monster to no end.

Ashlyn would recognize that voice anywhere. *Karina!* She started to say her name, but nothing more than a gurgle came out.

"Karina," she tried again and succeeded. Despite everything, Ashlyn was beyond happy that her sister was still alive. *So we can die together.*

The monster put her down. Well, not exactly. More like dropped her to the cement floor like she was a sack of dirt.

"Ashlyn, can you hear me? Can you see me?"

She followed the voice, and true enough, there was her sister chained to a wall. As Ashlyn looked at her younger sister, the monster put a collar around her neck.

"Why are you doing this?" she asked in a weak voice.

That was the first time he'd looked at her since he'd pulled her out of the van. It was a stranger's face. She didn't recognize him at all.

"Because you're no better than the rest," he snapped, standing up. He looked at the other women around the room. "Meet my new pet, Number Six," he declared before storming away.

Pet? Number six? Which meant five other women were inside that strange room. She had so many questions, so many emotions, yet her body gave up, and Ashlyn blacked out. She welcomed the nothingness.

32

Ashlyn came to feeling horrible. Every part of her being hurt. She felt like a bus had run over her a couple of times.

And then she heard a soft voice next to her. "Ashlyn, please wake up."

It was her sister.

She did as was asked, forcing her eyes open, which wasn't that easy. "Karina," she breathed through a busted lip.

"Here. Drink some water," her sister offered.

Ashlyn did as she was told again. After all that had happened, following orders, and not thinking about anything sounded like the best course of action. Although it felt nice, her mouth protested being forced to work. She started to sob, suddenly feeling overwhelmed.

"Hey, hey. Calm down," Karina said, embracing her tentatively.

Like Ashlyn, Karina looked beaten up, with cuts and bruises in various stages of healing, but she was alive. She was alive. Ashlyn had found her, although not in the manner she'd hoped for. This way, she hadn't actually managed to help anyone.

We will die here.

"I'm so sorry, Karina," she managed to choke out through the sobs.

"Nothing to feel sorry about, Ash. This is not your fault," her sister was quick to reassure. "It's all mine."

"I don't understand," she said, searching her sister's face. "How could any of this be your fault?"

"It's Paul."

Ashlyn stared at her sister. "Paul? He's the one behind this?"

Karina nodded. "He's a lunatic. But don't worry. We'll be all right. We'll get out of here somehow."

Ashlyn forced herself to calm down, and that was when she noticed the other women who were trapped, chained in this hell hole. Four more, to be precise.

They had all been clearly mistreated, and seeing them brought fresh tears to her eyes.

You need to be stronger than this to survive.

"Why are we here?" Ashlyn asked, looking at her sister and the other women.

"I don't know, not really," Karina replied. "I thought I was the one he wanted. I'm not sure why he grabbed you too."

"Are you sure? I think he's been following me for months. Today—was it today?" Ashlyn frowned, but it hurt so she tried to relax her face. "Whatever, he followed me when I left my house. I thought it was Mason…" She began to panic again, her breath coming in uneven gasps as she remembered everything. "I thought Mason was the one who kidnapped all of you…"

"Who's Mason?" one of the women asked.

"Her husband," Karina answered, without looking over at her. Instead her eyes were on Ashlyn. "Why would you think Mason would do this?"

"Because... well, he doesn't like you and he's controlling and obsessive and he always locks himself in the basement, but I didn't find any evidence of you all being there. All I found was—" Ashlyn stopped short.

"What did you find?" Karina arched a brow. "Obviously you didn't find us, so what was it, Ash?"

"BDSM porn," Ashlyn said, her voice barely a whisper.

Karina snickered. "Interesting. Giving or receiving?"

Ashlyn's brow furrowed. "What do you mean?"

"Was the man in the video giving or receiving the punishment in the video you saw?"

Wincing, Ashlyn replied, "Giving."

Karina nodded. "That seems about right. I should have known he would be into that. I'm just surprised he never hurt you."

Ashlyn's mind flashed back to that one night on the couch where he had.

She must not have hidden her thoughts very well because a moment later, Karina said, "He did, didn't he? I'm going to kill him."

"How? We're stuck here," Ashlyn replied, her voice full of regret.

"We'll figure it out," Karina replied.

Over the next couple of hours, they all talked to one another. The other women talked about themselves and how they'd ended up down there.

They had been grabbed from the streets, drugged with something they believed was chloroform, only to awaken down in this basement, where Paul abused them.

Only Karina's story differed. Paul had threatened to kill all the others if Karina didn't come with him. At first Karina hadn't believed him, but then he'd shown her video proof and the next thing she knew, he had grabbed her and tossed her in the back of the van. She'd screamed and banged on the sides but, obviously, no one had come to her rescue.

Hearing all their stories and about their times with Paul was unbearable, but Ashlyn knew falling apart wouldn't help, especially once he returned, so she endured. Deep down, she knew she would survive this. She had to, and so did Karina. There was no way she would allow their parents to lose both their daughters to this monster. Her determination was stronger than anything else. Still, she didn't understand what Paul's end goal was.

All of the women were adamant about certain things though. Paul had no mercy, and he always returned to them, no matter what.

"Although there was a time that I believed we were alone for at least a few days," Olga provided.

"Where was he?" Ashlyn asked.

"We're not sure. He was angry when he returned, and his arm was bandaged up."

Ashlyn's gaze went to Karina's. "You don't think..." she let her words trail off.

"That he's the one who broke into your house?" Karina finished the thought.

Ashlyn nodded.

"Maybe. He used to be really good with tech stuff, and he liked to break into places just to prove he could. Probably how he got around your alarm system." Karina seemed to think about it. "Didn't Mason give the cops a sketch of the guy, though?"

"He did. I haven't gotten a good look at Paul though. It could be the same guy."

"I never did see the sketch. Maybe I should have, and we wouldn't be in this predicament." Karina sighed. "You know, you met him once, about four years ago."

"I don't remember," Ashlyn said.

Karina looked uncomfortable. "Remember that night I called you because I was drunk in a bar, and I'd gotten into a fight with someone?"

Ashlyn thought back and slowly nodded.

"You jumped all over me, telling me it was a stupid thing to do. Well, Paul saw you that night and he heard what you said to me. He thought you were a snooty bitch."

"Okay?" Ashlyn couldn't see how his overhearing her would lead to him kidnapping all these women, let alone Karina and herself.

"Right, so the rest of the time I was with him, he'd make comments about you. It was one of the reasons why I finally kicked him to the curb and decided to get my act together."

Ashlyn still didn't understand. "So? What does that have to do with all of this?"

"Think about it, Ash. You said he's been following you for months, but I think it's been longer, honestly. He broke into your house. I think he's obsessed with you. It's you that he's wanted all along. The others were just substitutes for you."

Ashlyn's jaw dropped. She didn't even know him! "Wait... but then why grab you?"

"Maybe because I could identify him," Karina suggested. "Maybe he thought I would remember how obsessed he was with you and go to the cops when you went missing. I don't know."

"That's insane!" Ashlyn said, beginning to feel even more frightened than she was before. She looked at the other women and frowned. "I'm so sorry you all have been brought into this."

Amanda, who had been there the longest, just looked at her, her eyes dead. She was almost catatonic, and barely registered anything. Olga had shared that Amanda had attempted to escape once, and had even made it up to the main house, but because she was physically weak from being held for so long, he'd easily subdued her and returned her to the dungeon room. That was when he'd put the collars on them. Amanda hadn't been the same since then.

None of them really knew how much time had gone by since they'd each been taken. Ashlyn had informed them all that several months had passed since Amanda's disappearance, according to the news reports she'd watched, and Amanda hadn't taken it well.

Natalie hadn't spoken much either, keeping mostly to herself, slightly away from the others. And by the way Olga eyed her, it was obvious something was off with her as well.

"We're never getting out of here, are we?" Olga said. The look in her eyes said she truly believed that.

Ashlyn could only pray that she was wrong.

33

Ashlyn had no idea how much time had passed since Paul had imprisoned her in the round room with the others.

Has anyone noticed I'm missing yet? Has Mason? It was constantly on the tip of her tongue to ask Paul, but she never did. She was sure he would lie, anyway.

Her parents must be worried sick. *Has he done something to them? Has he done something to Mason?*

She didn't dare share her fears with Karina because she was worried her impulsiveness could get her into more trouble than she already was. She wasn't like Karina. She wasn't as strong as she was. Karina seemed hardened to everything. She didn't cry. She didn't even scream when Paul hurt her. She just stared daggers at him the entire time he "played" with her. That was what he called it.

He was a monster, the stuff nightmares were made of. He treated them like prized toys with Ashlyn as his favorite. Not that his treatment was nice; it was as far from it as you could get or even imagine. He was obsessed with her hair; it was the only thing left unmarred by him. The rest of her body had marks from his abuse. All of them did.

That first time he came down to the room had been a memory she never wanted to relive, though she had every time she closed her eyes. What he'd done to her—what he'd done to them all—was something she wanted to forget and tried not to think about, yet knew it would haunt her for the rest of her days.

"Good evening, my pets," Paul called out before they could actually see him, snapping her from her thoughts.

He used a remote from his pocket to chain them to a wall. He liked to start their evenings that way. He got off on control, and he liked to constantly show them that he was in charge.

Paul strode forward and grabbed Ashlyn's arm. "You," he growled as he unchained her. "Uppity bitch, thinking she's better than me," he muttered as he dragged her out of the round room and into the hallway. He opened a door and thrust her inside. "You and that fucker who shot me are going to pay for all of this." He slammed a fist into Ashlyn's face.

Ashlyn heard the crunch as her nose began to gush blood. She couldn't breathe, the pain was so intense. She didn't hear much more after that and she tried to tune out what he was saying and doing to her body. Eventually, he finished, and he dragged her from the cot he'd tossed her on, to her feet. He shoved her into the hallway.

"You're a disgusting parasite, and you're going to rot in hell," Ashlyn spat at him.

Paul grabbed her by the neck, squeezing hard as he slammed her back against the cement wall. "What did you just say to me?" he demanded, eyes wild, glazed with fury.

It wasn't a pretty sight. Although she knew she should be terrified of him, considering what he'd done to her—to all of them—she wasn't.

This must be what a mental breakdown feels like.

"You heard me," she replied defiantly.

He slapped her so hard her brain felt scrambled, but that didn't make her regret her words. More to the point, she smiled.

That certainly put him in a peculiar mood.

"You're a misbehaving whore," he said, continuing to choke her.

Knowing she'd managed to rattle him only made her grin bigger. It didn't matter that she could hardly breathe. Death would be better than enduring any more of this torture.

Seeing her grinning, he cussed and dragged her back to the circular room and reattached the chain. He used the remote to force her to return to her place against the wall. *Her place.* She hated that way of thinking.

"You think you're so smart."

Ashlyn said nothing, but she did her best to smirk at him.

"For that disobedience, I'm going to take your punishment out on your sister," he threatened.

No, no, no. She'd fucked up. She hadn't wanted him to go after Karina. She'd wanted him to kill her. To end her pain. To end her suffering. But Paul had chosen a different way to get at her.

Ashlyn started to cry, apologizing to Karina over and over.

Karina remained strong, brave, and unrelenting though.

And once he finished punishing her, he walked up to

Ashlyn and punched her in the stomach. "Fuck you, bitch. Next time, I'll use a ball-gag on you."

Ashlyn gasped and fell to her knees. She wouldn't survive a next time.

As Ashlyn watched him walk away, she hoped that he would have a heart attack and die in front of them. *Damn psychopath.* She cursed the day Karina had met him. She cursed the day Mason hadn't managed to kill him.

Usually while Paul was gone, Ashlyn and the others had relative freedom to move about the room. But when he decided to punish them, it was different. Today he'd left them as they were, all chained to the wall. They couldn't move except enough to sit on the floor against the wall or take a few steps forward. She knew from what the others had said that he called it a lesson. A lesson in humility and obedience.

Ashlyn looked at Karina and started to cry.

"I'm okay, Ash," her sister tried to reassure her as blood trickled down her face.

Naturally, her words made it worse, and Ashlyn cried even harder. She was crying out of anger, frustration, and desperation as if she were out of pain. Perhaps Karina was all right or at least saying that to calm her, but Ashlyn definitely wasn't.

No matter how hard she tried, she saw no way out of this. No escape from this hell. She was succumbing more to despair no matter how much she struggled not to.

We are going to die here.

She only hoped Paul would die before them.

34

Ashlyn was deeply worried about her sister. She was beaten up, and there was nothing she could do to help her or clean her wounds.

They had to find a way to break free, but how? If only there were a way to break that damn remote of his or steal it. He was very careful with it, always keeping it inside his pocket. Ashlyn wasn't that good a thief. The only time she had tried to steal something—from a store, on a dare—she'd gotten caught.

What if he's distracted by one of the others? There were more of them than him. Surely, they could find a way.

If only they weren't chained to the wall. She would be able to think more clearly if she could walk around for a bit and have something to eat. She was already starting to get hungry, and there was no telling when he would return.

Don't think about food. The longer he stays away, the better.

Ashlyn could feel her limbs numbing, slowly checking out. They had to get out of there before her soul broke down into a million pieces without any chance of repair. Because once all of this became normal, it was game over.

The whole place smelled bad, but Ashlyn forced herself not to think about it. After a while, it was apparent he was not coming back to release them from the wall.

"I don't feel so good," Charlene muttered as her head lolled forward.

"Charlene, hey. Wake up," Olga yelled.

"What's the matter with her?" Ashlyn asked, concerned.

"She has diabetes," Olga explained.

Oh, no. "Does Paul know that?"

Olga looked at her as though she'd just asked a stupid question. Even if he did, he wouldn't care. That much was obvious.

"What can we do?" Ashlyn didn't know much about that disease, but even she was aware of how dangerous it was and that a person could end up in a coma and die if not treated properly.

"I need to eat something," Charlene muttered.

What could they do? They were all chained to the wall. The only person who could help her was Paul. *Damn Paul.*

Realizing she was fuming instead of trying to solve the current problem, she focused on Charlene. The poor girl was clearly slipping in and out of consciousness, muttering something as though having a bad dream.

We are all living inside it.

"We need to call him back. That's the only way," Ashlyn advised them. Without Paul, she feared they would lose Charlene.

"Hey, asshole!" Karina yelled, banging with her chains against the metal ring that echoed around them.

"Subtle," Ashlyn replied dryly.

"We don't have time for subtle," her sister pointed out.

"Help! We need help!" Olga joined in.

They screamed, begged, and threatened for what felt like hours.

Ashlyn feared their pleas couldn't be heard wherever Paul had gone off to. *Please, God, help us. Help her,* she prayed.

"Fuck it, I think this place is soundproofed," Karina said. Despite being savagely beaten, she was putting up the effort like the rest of them.

"I think so too but we have to keep trying," Ashlyn replied.

So, they persisted.

Eventually, Paul appeared at the door. "Did you learn your lesson, or do I need to continue your fasting?" he asked smugly.

"Release Charlene now," Karina ordered.

Paul looked at her, his eyes narrowed and menacing. "Excuse me?"

"You will feed her, or she'll die," Karina said.

He turned to look at Charlene. "What did you do to her?" he demanded, outraged.

"This is on you, asshole," Karina argued. "She's having a bad attack of hypoglycemia."

"She's diabetic?" he asked with a disgusted expression on his face. He might as well have asked if she had leprosy.

"Please, Paul, you have to feed her," Ashlyn said before things escalated further, forgetting about her pride at the moment. "She will die without your help. She is at your mercy. We all are."

Karina sent her a look, but she ignored it. There was nothing she wouldn't say or do to help this poor girl.

Paul looked at her for a full excruciating moment, his

eyes raking over her with lust, before resuming a bored expression. "Fine," he relented. "Feed her," he commanded, using the remote to free their chains.

Ashlyn stumbled since her legs had gone completely numb.

"Thank you," Olga told him, rushing toward Charlene.

Ashlyn was giving Charlene some water when Paul turned and walked out the door again.

As Ashlyn focused on helping Charlene, she determined to remain strong. They would find a way out. They would survive this. They would defeat Paul.

Even if it meant killing him in the process.

35

It was difficult to nurse Charlene back to health because Paul refused to get her any medicine. Mostly, they gathered up anything from their meals that weren't cheap carbohydrates or fruits and gave it to her to eat and gave her part of their water rations as well. It was a sacrifice, considering where they were, but they all did it, and gladly. Her blood sugar stabilized, and she started to feel much better. She looked better as well.

"I wish I could stay sick forever," Charlene confessed.

Amanda nodded, and whispered, "Me too. I want to die."

Ashlyn understood the sentiment. Paul had refused to touch Charlene while she was sick, as though afraid he would get diabetes from her, as if it were a virus he could catch.

Thoughts of Mason suddenly filled her mind. She felt guilty for focusing on Mason as the bad guy, and she regretted how she'd left things between them. She still didn't understand the BDSM porn thing and wondered if he was cheating on her, but he wasn't a serial kidnapper. He wasn't actually an abuser of women. Well, at least she didn't think so.

Wallowing in sorrow and self-pity, thinking about her marriage and if Mason was cheating on her wasn't an option at the moment. Figuring out how to escape was. She owed all these women that much. If that meant sacrificing herself for them, then that's what she would do. She would gladly offer herself in exchange for their lives. Ashlyn wouldn't allow Charlene or anyone else to die here.

She understood why she was so willing to be the sacrificial lamb. She was the one Paul was obsessed with. They were only here because he hadn't had the guts to grab her first. He'd said as much one of the first times he'd assaulted her. She felt responsible even though she had no way of knowing about his obsession. Sure, Karina had known, so she'd taken steps to rid him from her life. But here he was. Back with a vengeance. Ashlyn felt bad that Karina seemed to blame herself for his actions.

Paul was a monster. But that wasn't Karina's fault. She couldn't have anticipated that he would lose his mind and kidnap a bunch of women who all kind of looked like them just because he was obsessed with her sister. No sane person would do such a thing. The guy was clearly deranged.

They would survive this hell, and Paul would pay for all he'd done to them. Ashlyn knew that Mason would make sure of that. That was what kept her going. That was what helped her endure all the torture Paul put her through.

WHEN THEY HEARD Paul coming down the hall, they tensed immediately, knowing what would follow.

As it turned out, he wasn't alone.

"Do you like my playroom?" Paul said as he shoved someone in front of him.

He almost sounded like an excited boy showing off his cool toys. Ashlyn shuddered.

"Has he brought a friend?" Karina muttered.

Ashlyn frowned. The lights were dim, and she couldn't see who was with Paul. "Shush," she murmured.

"I think we might need a little more light for you to see all my beauties," Paul said.

A moment later the room lit up.

And then Ashlyn's gaze focused on the new person, and she recognized them. "Oh, no," she breathed as her whole body went numb.

36

Ashlyn went pale knowing this wouldn't end well, especially since Paul was bragging about the secret playhouse they were standing in.

Her eyes dragged over the man standing with a gun to his back. His hands were bound, and he had a black eye. Blood trickled down the side of his face from a wound on his temple. Ashlyn's heart raced. She'd never seen him looking so bad.

Mason.

What the hell was he doing here?

"I'm especially proud of one of my toys in particular," Paul continued, and started to lead Mason over toward her.

Ashlyn practically stopped breathing. She didn't want her husband seeing her like this. She wanted to hide from Mason's gaze. But there was nowhere for her to go. "Please, no," she begged.

It was enough. Mason had heard her, and he looked up, his eyes widening. "Ashlyn!"

Big mistake.

"No!" Paul roared. "Six! That toy is named Six!"

"You fucking bastard! That's my wife!" Mason yelled at him, struggling with the bindings on his hands. "Let her the fuck go!"

"Why would I do that?" Paul challenged. "She's mine. They all are. My playthings."

"You're fucking insane. I should have killed you when I found you in my house!"

Paul sneered. "It was so easy to break in. I can get in anywhere."

Mason lunged at him, leading with his chest, but Paul punched him in the face, and Mason dropped to his knees.

"You shouldn't have followed my van. You should have left well enough alone. Now you're in my playroom and you won't be able to share what you know with anyone."

"You're not going to get away with this. I'm going to kill you."

Paul laughed, which seemed to infuriate Mason even more as he yanked on his hands, obviously trying to bust through the zip ties holding his wrists.

"Aw, you really think you have a say in this?" Paul mocked him.

Mason glanced at her, his eyes full of rage and regret at the situation.

Ashlyn whispered, "I'm sorry," as tears slid down her cheeks.

"I think we've been down here long enough, my friend." Paul dragged Mason to his feet.

"I'm not your fucking friend, you lunatic! Let my wife and these other women go!" Mason roared again.

Paul ignored him. "Now, I think it's time to conclude our tour. There's one more place I want to show you." He grabbed Mason's forearms, pushing him toward the hallway again.

All the women were in a panic now, not just Ashlyn. It was as though the spell were finally broken and they could react.

"Let go of me," Mason yelled.

"Please, don't leave us here," Charlene sobbed.

"Please help us," Natalie joined in.

"No," Ashlyn screamed as she heard a door shut. She knew Mason wasn't going to make it out of there alive. *Oh, God, please help, please help us,* she prayed.

"What are you doing?" Mason's voice carried down the hall. "Wait... Stop... I've got money..."

Ashlyn heard the gun go off and then Mason screamed.

"Please, stop... How much do you want... I can—" His words were cut off by another gun shot.

Ashlyn began crying uncontrollably.

There were three more gun shots.

Each shot tore a hole in her own heart. Mason was dead because of her. She might as well have pulled the trigger herself since he'd come to this place to rescue her. Somehow, she'd led him here to his death. She'd killed him.

When Paul opened the door and returned to the circular room, he was covered in blood. The worst part was that he was smiling. He was practically giddy after murdering Ashlyn's husband.

He was a monster. And he would never stop. Not even Mason could stop him. What hope did she and the others have?

37

Paul had murdered her husband. He'd killed him with no remorse at all. In fact, Paul looked happy at what he'd done, which sickened her. Ashlyn hoped that one day he would experience all the pain and suffering he had inflicted upon others.

He killed Mason. Those words were on repeat inside her head. He'd killed him and was happy about it.

Paul muttered something about finally being free to do what he wanted with Ashlyn. He walked toward her with a big smile. "We'll celebrate together in a little while, but first I need to teach my other toys how to behave better," he said as he moved toward Natalie.

He unhooked her from the wall and dragged her down the hallway. Natalie screamed as he shut the door behind them.

After he was done with Natalie, he came after each of them, leaving Ashlyn for last, as he'd promised.

Seeing Mason's body on the floor, knowing the only

reason he was even in this place was because of her, was a torture beyond anything she could have ever imagined. She did her best to keep her eyes off Mason, closing them tightly as Paul abused her.

Rest in peace, Mason, she prayed. *I'm so sorry for believing it was you.*

Why didn't Mason go to the police? Why did he come here? Why did he confront Paul instead of finding a way to rescue them? All of these questions played on Ashlyn's mind. Questions she'd probably never know the answers to. She wished she could go back in time and fix things. Of course, life didn't work like that.

The awfulness of what had taken place turned her stomach inside out. She was to blame. Mason's death was her fault. These women being kidnapped was her fault. All of it was on her.

This is all my fault. Ashlyn sobbed. She'd brought Paul to their doorstep. If she'd trusted Mason, told the police about being followed when they were at the station, told the police about the van on the street… Mason would still be alive.

After Paul had finished with them for the day, he left, humming to himself. He laughed, saying good night to Mason as though he were alive and sitting in that room, not dead on the floor.

He'd completely lost his mind.

That was worrisome. If he was spiraling out of control, then there was no telling what he could do next. That was the biggest problem. Now they knew he was capable of anything. If he could kill someone then laugh about it, then he could kill them all tomorrow without a problem and start kidnapping another bunch of women.

Ashlyn couldn't let that happen, and not just because she

wanted to live. She couldn't allow anyone else to suffer at his hands. She just couldn't. Enough was enough.

"It can't go on like this," Karina said, mirroring her thoughts. "We have to do something."

"I agree," Ashlyn added. "We have to stop him."

"What can we do?" Charlene questioned. "We don't have anything, no weapons." She pointed at her naked body.

"And let's face it, we are all exhausted," Olga spoke up as well. "Beaten pretty good, and frankly speaking, not in our best shape since... being here."

"None of that matters." Karina was adamant. "It's up to us to save ourselves. Mason tried, and ended up dead. If we don't get out of here, we're going to end up just like him."

We need to stop him so we can tell others what he did. What he did to Mason. He deserves justice.

"He'll kill you if he hears you speaking like this," Natalie said, cowering in fear.

"You'll rat on us?" Karina challenged.

"What do you think?" Natalie threw back in a spiteful tone.

"Okay, so we are all on the same page," Karina replied, as though satisfied with her reply.

"I'm afraid of him," Amanda confessed.

"We all are, but what's the alternative?" Ashlyn pointed out.

"He'll kill us, no matter what," Karina added.

Natalie nodded. Ashlyn took that to mean she was on board.

"So, what can we do?" Charlene asked.

"Whatever it is, it has to be a group activity. None of us can defeat him solo," Ashlyn insisted.

"What do you mean?" Karina, Amanda, and Olga asked at the same time.

"We have to all work together," Ashlyn replied with a small shrug. "Paul is stronger than us, so someone needs to distract him while the others rush at him together."

"But we need to do something about that damn remote first so he can't pull these chains tight and make us stand against the wall again," Karina pointed out as she rattled the chain attached to her collar.

They all nodded.

"What about the gun?" Natalie added.

"He hasn't brought it down here before. Just when he brought Mason. Maybe he'll leave it elsewhere since he thinks he's got us under control," Ashlyn suggested.

"True," Karina replied.

"I don't think he wants us dead," Amanda whispered. "If he did, he'd have already killed us."

"That's comforting, I guess," Charlene voiced what was on all their minds.

"So, we are in agreement? We go at him together?" Karina insisted.

"Yes, together," Ashlyn agreed.

"Together," Olga said, and there was resolve in her eyes.

"Together," Charlene said, although there was fear in her eyes.

"Okay, together," Amanda added.

The only one who wavered was Natalie.

Amanda nodded as though coming to some decision and looked at Natalie. "Together, Natalie."

And for the first time, Natalie sounded strong and resolute as she agreed. "Fine. Together."

Ashlyn was glad, because they would need all their strength and courage if they wanted to do this.

They talked for a while about the best course of action, but in hushed voices, since they feared Paul could come back and overhear their plans. They were all more paranoid about him after Amanda's attempted escape, because he'd beat all of them for hours after he'd returned her to them. None of them wanted that to happen this time. They felt they all needed to be able to get free, not just one of them. What had just happened to Ashlyn's husband made them feel more on edge as well.

"We need to convince him we're so rattled by what he did that we fear him now completely, and play along with everything without resistance," Karina coached.

"That doesn't sound too difficult," Olga said dryly.

"I know, right?" Karina replied in the same manner.

"However, you have to be more careful," Olga said. "If you turn your attitude 180, he might start suspecting something."

"Good point," Karina agreed. "Maybe I need to continue giving him lip, if nothing else." Her lips twisted. "You know, our relationship was always contentious. He always got off on me being mouthy to him. Granted, he wasn't ever violent before, not like this, but yeah, he was rough. I used to like it. God, I hate admitting that."

"This isn't your fault," Olga assured her. "Something's the matter with him. Something's wrong in his brain. Maybe it's the drugs or the booze. Who knows?"

"Yeah, maybe he's got a mental disorder. Either way, it's not your fault. It's his," Natalie added.

"We can do this. We just need to be smart about it, right?" Karina said.

The women nodded in agreement, except one. Ashlyn wasn't sure about any of this. She wasn't sure about anything anymore. The more she thought about it, the more doubts she had. Although she knew this was their only shot, part of her wanted to pump the brakes on this plan of theirs.

That was kind of ironic, having Natalie and Amanda on board and her on the fence.

Karina, as though sensing something was brewing inside her, ushered her to one side of the room, as far as their chains would allow anyway, to have a more private conversation.

"What's the matter, Ash?" she asked.

Ashlyn decided to be completely honest with her sister. She owed her that much after being the sole reason she'd found herself in this mess in the first place. "I don't know if I can go through with this."

There, I said it.

Karina looked at her long and hard, as though trying to read her mind before answering. "Do you not think it will work?"

"Of course I do," Ashlyn replied instantly.

"Then what is it?" Karina insisted.

"I don't know if I can have anyone else's death on my conscience," she replied, exhaling heavily.

"Excuse me?" Karina looked lost.

"Mason died because of me. If anything happened to any one of you, I wouldn't be able to bear it."

"You're talking nonsense."

"No, I'm not. This all happened because I was blind, because I dismissed things that I should not have. And then I went a step further and thought Mason was behind it all." Her voice hitched at that. "If I had been paying attention to what was actually happening and not focusing on the bad guy being Mason, then he wouldn't be dead now."

Karina gave her a hug and tears streamed down her face. Her sister held her for a bit until she regained control of herself.

"First of all," Karina started again once they parted, "you didn't kill Mason. Paul did."

"I know, but—"

"No, no, listen to me. He killed him, end of story," Karina insisted.

"I know he killed him." She was not an idiot. "I still feel guilty that he was here in the first place, trying to rescue me."

"That's not on you. Mason made a choice. He chose to come here without backup, without calling the cops. He had to have had proof or at least suspected Paul was behind all of this to end up here. It's not your fault Mason wanted to play hero and be the badass he thought he was. His death is a tragedy, but you have nothing to do with it. It's all on Paul, and honestly, it's on Mason too."

Well, when she put it that way, it did make sense.

"Second of all, what is the alternative?"

"What do you mean?"

"If we don't do this, what can we do?" Karina challenged.

"I don't know."

"Exactly, and that's because this is our only shot. Paul is not going to let us go. We're going to die, Ash. Eventually Paul will get bored with us and kill us off." Karina emphasized each word. "We need to do this to survive, because if we remain down here, he *will* kill us. We will end up just like Mason. You understand?"

"I understand," Ashlyn replied.

"It's do or die," Karina insisted.

"Do or die," Ashlyn repeated and let those words sink in.

Do or die. Ashlyn had no idea what would happen, but no matter what, this had to end.

"Do or die," she repeated with more confidence.

38

They had all agreed that they would put their plan into motion the next time Paul returned.

He surprised them all and appeared that evening.

Now her heart beat like crazy, but Ashlyn reined in all her fears. This had to be done. As Karina said, there was no other way.

They were all chained against the wall, and she shared one last look with Karina before casting her gaze downward. They were playing the part, after all.

It's now or never.

If they did exactly as they discussed, they had a decent chance to end this horror today. The good news was that they would have the element of surprise. The bad news was that none of them knew who would be chosen.

Ashlyn was determined to defeat Paul. He'd made a huge mistake in his depraved greed. He was only one man, and they were many. That was exactly what would be his downfall. They had strength in numbers, she repeated like a mantra.

So, when he started making decisions about his first pick, Ashlyn played it cool and acted as though what he was doing was the most natural thing in the world.

They all waited, holding their breaths for him to make the final decision. And then Ashlyn felt her chain coming loose.

He picked me.

Without a conscious decision, Ashlyn acted. She rushed toward him and then jumped, making him drop the remote before he could send them all flying backwards toward the wall, which was the goal from the start. She didn't stop there. She couldn't. Ashlyn started scratching his face, hitting, biting, letting her survival instincts kick in because she was fighting for her life.

Then she heard the most beautiful thing. "I got it!" Karina yelled.

Unfortunately, that made her relax a bit, which was a huge mistake.

In the next instant, Paul hit her so hard that she fell to the floor.

"I'll kill you, you stupid whore," he boomed, coming at her.

But Ashlyn had still managed to buy her sister enough time to get the remote and free all the other women, who in turn charged at Paul as one.

As all the women started hitting their tormentor, Karina came from behind and looped a length of her chain around his neck and started to pull at it, choking him. The other women jumped on him, preventing him from taking the chain off. After Ashlyn regained her balance, she joined in, trying to restrain him.

He fought them tooth and nail. He struggled, tried to fend them off, but there were just too many of them. He couldn't fight them all off.

At some point, he tried to shout, but the chain around his neck prevented him from doing so.

"How do you like having a chain around your neck, asshole?" Karina spat as she pulled.

Paul tried to fend her off and get the chain off, but all the women pulled his hands away, making him fall down. Eventually, he lost the fight.

But even after he fell to the floor, they continued to beat him. He'd tormented them for so long that they all wanted— needed —to make sure he was actually defeated.

"Stop, stop. We don't want to kill the guy," Karina cautioned at some point.

It was as though the spell was broken and they all stopped in unison, taking a step away from him. Paul lay motionless on the floor, moving in and out of consciousness, beaten up and bleeding profusely. He looked pathetic.

Ashlyn looked at him, marred with blood, and felt nothing other than vindication. He'd finally gotten a small taste of what he'd put them through, and that was right. That was just.

She was pretty winded and needed a moment to calm herself. She wasn't the only one. It appeared they all needed a moment to realize they'd won. The atmosphere instantly changed inside the room when that knowledge finally sank in.

They all looked at one another and smiled.

Karina started to bark orders, needing to make sure he was properly restrained.

But Ashlyn still needed an additional moment to herself. *We actually did it.* Part of her feared this was a hallucination or something. Yet the thick, heavy chain around her neck suggested she was not dreaming.

That was when Paul looked up at her. "My beauty," he said slowly.

She looked at him without responding.

"You'll always be mine."

"Excuse me?" Ashlyn countered.

"If you help me get up, we can run away together. We can have it all."

"What?" Ashlyn knew she was repeating herself, yet it couldn't be helped.

"We can be together always. Just you and me."

"What about the other women?" Ashlyn asked to satisfy her curiosity.

"We'll kill them."

Ashlyn could not believe her ears. Did he really think she would run off with him? The man was delusional.

She leaned forward to make sure he heard her next words loud and clear. "First of all, I am not yours. And second, things like you are not allowed to speak." And to prove her point, she kicked him in the mouth, knocking him unconscious. It hurt her foot, but it was worth it.

Karina cheered, approaching. "That crazy son of a bitch," she commented with a shake of her head, mimicking Ashlyn's thoughts perfectly.

"That felt so good," Ashlyn admitted.

Her sister chuckled. "I'll bet."

"Now, let's see how we're going to take these chains off our necks."

Ashlyn nodded. "Sounds like a plan."

As the majority of them looked about for anything that could be used as a tool, Karina looked Paul over to make sure he was down for the count.

Ashlyn felt elated. Still in slight disbelief.

We did it.

It felt great standing up to Paul. He was not stronger than her. She'd proven that.

She was finally free; they all were. But this was far from over. Looking at the bleeding bastard, she knew the real battle with the trial, and everything had only just begun.

Yet she was looking forward to it because Paul deserved to rot in jail, and Ashlyn would make sure to send him there if she couldn't send him to hell instead.

39

Karina managed to free all of them with a piece of metal she extracted from the remote control. It felt good not to have that collar around her neck anymore, to be able to walk around completely free and leave the basement. Ashlyn would never again doubt her sister's skills. She was a rock star as far as Ashlyn was concerned. They were all free because of her. And once they were all free, they made sure Paul wasn't.

Charlene immediately covered herself in a sheet, which reminded Ashlyn they would definitely need some clothes before anything else.

They'd lived without their dignity, among other things, for far too long. They needed to find theirs. She hoped one of the rooms held what he'd taken from them. Sure enough, in the final room in the hallway, Ashlyn found their clothes.

"Here, take these." She waved a set of clothes toward Charlene.

She once again looked a bit sickly, and Ashlyn thought it would be best to try to stabilize her to the best of their ability before the paramedics came, which she had to call first. How she was going to do that, she wasn't sure yet. But she'd figure it out.

"Let's go," Ashlyn said once they were all dressed. She yanked open the door to the steps she recalled Paul bringing her down. At the top was a door and she opened it to find they were in a kitchen.

Natalie and Amanda had come along with them, while Olga and Karina stayed in the circular room to watch over Paul.

"He's tied up. He won't be going anywhere," Charlene pointed out. "We should stay together."

It was obvious Charlene felt anxious, and Ashlyn understood. She, too, felt uneasy. But at the moment her priority was to get some food in Charlene.

"There's the fridge." She pointed. "Go eat whatever you want. I'll see what I can find in this place."

Natalie and Amanda stayed with Charlene. Apparently, Ashlyn wasn't the only one concerned.

"Thank you," Charlene called as Ashlyn left the room.

"No problem," Ashlyn muttered as she began to look around. She needed to track down a phone.

I need to call the police, she stressed, turning the living room upside down. She didn't know if she'd find a cell phone, but she was hopeful. Those hopes were dashed when she found nothing but a TV remote.

And then it hit her. Maybe the house had a landline? It seemed to be an older home, so that was probable. She must have been in shock or something since that hadn't crossed her mind in the first place. Of course she was in shock. It would be ridiculous to assume otherwise.

Rushing back to the kitchen, where Charlene, Amanda,

and Natalie still ate by the open refrigerator, Ashlyn looked around the room, noticed the yellow phone on the wall and grabbed the receiver. She dialed 911 and waited.

"911 dispatch," the operator said.

"Oh, thank God." Ashlyn rushed to explain the situation. "But I have no idea where we are," she added.

"I can trace the call, ma'am. Are you sure you're safe? The police are on their way. Do I need to send rescue services as well?"

Ashlyn glanced at Charlene. "Yes, please."

"Okay. If you feel secure, you don't have to stay on the line. Police and rescue will be there shortly."

"Thank you," Ashlyn murmured. "I'm going to let the others know they're on their way," she told the three eating.

As she started back toward the door that led down to the circular room, she wavered on whether she should call her parents, but ruled against it. They would want to come immediately, but she couldn't bear seeing them. Besides, she wasn't even sure exactly where she was. Not right now. *Later,* she promised, feeling guilty that she was prolonging their pain.

With all that settled, she had another stroke of inspiration. Paul owned a gun, the gun he'd used to kill Mason. He hadn't had it on him. Perhaps she should look for it.

But then she realized that was a job for the police, and besides, she felt bone tired all of a sudden. As she went down the steps, all she wanted was for this to be over so she could lie down and sleep for a month straight.

And once I wake up, I will discover that Mason's alive and well and this was all a horrible nightmare.

Yeah, right.

As she reached the bottom step, she heard someone

behind her and, suddenly frightened, she turned to see Natalie. She let out a breath and said, "You scared me."

"Sorry."

It turned out that she too needed to make sure Paul was actually beaten, that this was not a dream but reality.

"The police are on their way," she informed her sister and Olga.

Natalie approached the chained Paul without a word and stared at him.

Ashlyn felt slightly uneasy, as though she was an intruder in a private moment. Natalie's expression was indecipherable, at least to her.

A moment later, Natalie landed a kick in Paul's face.

It looked as though she was going to do it again, so Ashlyn gently pulled her backward. "He can't hurt you anymore."

It felt like they didn't have to be down there anymore, because Karina had bound Paul well and attached his bindings to the chain on the wall, going as far as to leave him naked for good measure.

"Come on, Nat, let's go back upstairs," she said, causing Natalie to jump.

It was no wonder. They were all jumpy.

"Sorry, I didn't meant to startle you."

"It's fine," Natalie was quick to reassure, returning her gaze to Paul. "Do you think we will ever be able to escape this place?" she added after a pause.

That was a very good question. Ashlyn wondered about that herself. "I hope so," she replied honestly, "because at the end of the day, we all did what we had to, to survive."

The other woman nodded.

"Let's go upstairs," Ashlyn urged.

They all went upstairs and sat in the living room without talking, as though they all needed a moment or two to process this new reality, as they patiently waited for the police to arrive.

She couldn't quite remember when that happened, but after the calm came such a whirlwind of activity that she felt dazed. The police and ambulance came, accompanied by a pair of Tahoe detectives, and that buzz of activity, a full house of people, strangers, was in such contrast with everything else, to the way she was forced to live down in that basement, Ashlyn felt like running away and hiding from it all.

She had to force herself to remain calm. *You survived this far. You can manage to answer some questions and get a check-up from a doctor.* She was constantly giving herself a pep talk.

The paramedics treated Charlene and Amanda first, since they were in the poorest states, with Charlene having diabetes that had gone untreated for so long and Amanda being seriously underweight. It became obvious they were very concerned about their well-being the most, and they were rushed to the hospital. Charlene protested that she didn't want to go alone, seeing as she and Amanda were being loaded into separate ambulances, but Olga managed to calm her, promising they would all meet at the hospital later, so she finally agreed.

The rest of them were checked by the paramedics. They were all pretty starved, dehydrated, scared, and bruised. The good news was none of their wounds were life-threatening, so although they were advised to go to the hospital and have a more thorough examination, they wanted to stay for a bit and make sure Paul got exactly what he deserved.

"Where's the suspect?" a detective whose name she forgot asked.

"Bound and chained in the basement," Karina replied calmly.

The detective looked taken aback. "Could you repeat that?"

Ashlyn stood up from the sofa. "Come, I'll show you."

Karina went with them.

The two detectives—Detectives Ellison and North, she was reminded—looked baffled as Ashlyn led them down the corridor and into the circular room of torture.

"So, this is the asshole who kidnapped us, tortured, and raped us," Karina explained.

Detective Ellison approached the suspect, as he called him, and looked slightly impressed by their handiwork. He turned toward Karina and Ashlyn, inclining his head. "I apologize if I appeared to be a bit brazen upstairs."

Hearing voices, Paul started to stir, finally coming to. They'd beaten his ass up pretty good. He was already showing a lot of swelling and bruises.

"It's okay," Karina said generously.

"Do you mind telling me what happened?"

"To him, or in general?" Ashlyn asked for clarification.

"Shut the fuck up. Don't you dare open your mouth," Paul ordered.

"I knew I should have gagged him," Karina muttered, yet Ashlyn was sure she was the only one who heard her, since Paul was pretty loud.

"Let go of me. Unchain me." And then he turned toward the detectives. "Leave immediately. You're not allowed to be here."

It went without saying that they were unimpressed with his display of anger.

Ashlyn took a step toward him and slapped his face. The best part was neither of the detectives made a move to stop her.

As for Paul, that shut him right up.

"Haven't you learned by now that we don't take orders from you?" she threw in his face.

He looked startled for a moment but recovered quickly. He started raging then, pulling at his restraints, and threatening. "I'll kill you. I'll kill all of you for betraying me. You're done. You're nothing."

It was all in vain. He was no Hulk to break the bonds. He should have been impressed with himself. He'd built such a fine dungeon that not even he could escape from it.

"Hello again, Mr. Barns," the detective greeted. "Should have arrested you weeks ago, when I saw that sketch Mr. Adams made."

That enraged him, and Paul started to growl and thrash like an animal.

Ashlyn was shocked though. They had known it was Paul? How? Why had they allowed him to stay free?

Seeing that she wanted to speak, Detective North urged, "Let's take this conversation someplace else," as he pointed toward the exit.

"Yeah, we've seen enough," her partner agreed.

"I don't understand why you didn't arrest him if you knew he was the one who broke in."

"I was going to, believe me, but it was the same time your parents called in about your sister being missing and that took priority over a small case of breaking and entering... I meant to get back to him, but when I went looking, he'd disappeared. Now we know why," Detective North replied as they started to leave the room.

"What about him?" Karina wanted to know.

"It looks like he won't be going anywhere, but we'll send someone to keep watch," Detective Ellison reassured her.

On their way out, Ashlyn remembered to say, "You should know that Paul owns a gun, but I don't know what he did with it. He used it to kill my husband."

Detective Ellison paused. "When did he do that? I saw your husband four days ago when he came in demanding we find you."

Ashlyn felt tears fill her eyes. "I can't be sure. Yesterday? The day before?" She shook her head. "He's in there." She nodded toward a closed door.

"Okay. You're sure he's dead?"

Ashlyn nodded.

"I'm sorry for your loss," both detectives murmured.

"By the way, do you have the key?" Detective Ellison asked as he guided them back toward the stairs.

"Key?" Karina and Ashlyn asked almost simultaneously.

"To the chains."

"Nope," Karina replied, grinning.

Returning upstairs, they all sat in the living room and started sharing their stories with the detectives.

One by one, they spoke about how they were taken and what Paul did to them upon waking in the dungeon, including how they'd finally managed to free themselves.

"You weren't around, so we had to take matters into our hands," Karina jibed.

It was typical sass from her sister, and it made Ashlyn

smile. She knew it would help her get through the next several hours of questions. Hours she wasn't looking forward to.

40

Ashlyn felt kind of strange, as though in a daze, yet not quite. She was aware of everything that was happening but at the same time, there was a notion that all of this was happening to someone else, not to her. That feeling intensified as Paul was dragged out of the basement, arrested, and taken to jail. Ashlyn could hear him screaming and threatening as two police officers escorted him toward the police car, yet none of them went to watch.

She wanted that mental image of him being chained to the basement wall, beaten and bloody, to linger in her mind a little longer.

We won.

Once the detectives finished speaking with them, they were transported to the hospital. Ashlyn was treated for various cuts and bruises. She also had a broken rib, and in all the madness, she hadn't even felt it. The rest of the women fared pretty much the same, except for Karina, who had slightly more serious wounds. Paul had forcefully ripped out all her piercings, and some of the wounds were infected, so she was put on antibiotics and some other medications. Karina mourned her beautiful piercings, vowing to get new ones as soon as she was allowed.

They also learned Charlene and Amanda would be fine, at least physically. Ashlyn felt it was most important that they were all right. She had worried about them, especially since Charlene had diabetes and Paul refused to bring her insulin, so they'd barely managed to control her sugar levels on their own, but all that was in the past.

The atmosphere in the hospital was kind of strange. Word traveled fast about who they were, and all were in awe that six women managed to escape their tormentor. The women who worked in the hospital were especially kind to them. They were pampered and it felt nice. After all that had happened, such support and kindness left Ashlyn weeping.

Ashlyn knew they would leave the hospital in record time. Yet who would treat their psychological wounds? Who would fix their damaged souls?

It was hard to accept at times that it was all over. No matter what she told herself, her body was still battle-ready, as though waiting for Paul to return, and looking at Karina and the other women, she knew they felt the same way.

Ashlyn relaxed a bit after her parents came to visit. The reunion with Mom and Dad was a very heartfelt event. The four of them huddled together, hugging and crying, but eventually, the doctor ordered Ashlyn and Karina to return to their beds.

They did, but grudgingly.

"Hey, Doc, go fuck yourself," Karina said in a playful way.

Naturally, her mother was scandalized by her language.

"Maybe later. I'm doing rounds at the moment," he countered in the same manner.

They all laughed.

It felt good to laugh, although it felt strange at the same time. She would need time to get used to certain things after the nightmare they'd endured.

That's all over now.

They didn't speak with their parents about what happened within those walls underground. Ashlyn hoped they would never learn the depth of the horrors they had endured, but it was obvious Dad was prepared for murder. Even their mom, who was always kind and so full of forgiveness, said she hoped Paul would burn in hell, which was the worst thing ever, in her book.

Her parents had asked where Mason was, why he wasn't there at the hospital, and Ashlyn had broken down in tears as she explained that he'd found them, only for Paul to kill him. She'd probably never forgive herself for doubting him. She still had no idea if he'd really loved her or if he'd been cheating on her, but she'd unpack that at a later time.

As the evening wore on, Ashlyn and Karina did their best to calm their parents, knowing the real battles were up ahead of them and they all needed to be strong.

Ashlyn met the other parents as well. She felt awful. Although nobody told her she was the reason all this happened, she still felt guilty. It couldn't be helped.

Once they were deemed well enough, they were told they could all go home. In the meantime, the same two detectives who were in the house came to visit them and have another chat. Their parents had to leave the room while they spoke with the police again. They did that quite reluctantly, but Ashlyn thought that was for the best. They didn't need nightmares.

Karina spoke first, retelling her story from the beginning.

"That was when we knew we had to do something," Karina said before finishing with how they'd managed to take Paul down.

Once she finished, Ashlyn told her own story. Her story was a bit longer, starting with all her suspicions, first believing that Mason was having an affair, which led to her visiting Mason's mother. And then she shared what Mrs. Adams had told her about Mason and his sister, which led her to believe that he was guilty, only to be proven wrong when Paul forced her car off the road and then kidnapped her. It was important to her to share her guilt over thinking her own husband was behind everything.

If the pair of detectives thought she was an idiot for snooping around by herself without alerting the authorities, or for not noticing the van was the same as the one that was used to kidnap her sister and reporting it sooner, they didn't indicate it in any way. And she was grateful for that. She felt awful enough as it was.

In the middle of her story, Detective Ellison excused himself and left the room to take a call.

"Continue, please," Detective North encouraged.

"Charlene became extremely sick," Ashlyn continued, "and we did our best to help her."

Eventually, the other detective returned to the room. "Sorry to interrupt. I have some news that I think you need to hear."

Karina and Ashlyn looked at one another. Ashlyn thought of the worst. *Had Paul managed to escape? Were they in danger again?*

"What is it?" Karina prompted.

"Paul Barns committed suicide in his jail cell."

"How?" Karina asked.

The detective didn't hesitate to reply. "He slit his wrists with a makeshift blade he broke off the cot in his cell."

"Good," Karina replied.

Ashlyn realized she felt nothing upon hearing that news. There was no anger that he'd managed to escape justice. There was no relief that he wouldn't be able to hurt them again. There was only nothingness.

Nevertheless, she decided to send a thought for him, hoping he would get it.

Paul, rot in hell.

41

Four months had passed since Paul had committed suicide in jail like the coward he was. Ashlyn thought he'd gotten off easy, way too easy for what he did to them.

Fucking coward.

The media and the people in their community practically went mad. This was the biggest story that had ever affected their part of the world, or so it seemed. All the usual bullshit ensued. There were any number of people looking to get an inside scoop on their individual stories. Their heartache and pain was now the public's gossip.

Ashlyn's phone wouldn't stop ringing. All kinds of reporters and TV hosts tried to get an exclusive. Ashlyn refused to speak about it with anyone. That was something all six women were adamant about. They refused to speak about what happened to them publicly.

They wanted to carry on with their lives, not relive those moments over and over. At times, it was difficult since everyone was curious.

Karina was approached for a book deal. She was very graphic in her refusal. They didn't try again.

Having Mason dead made matters even worse. Especially with the way he'd died. The news studios wanted to turn him into some sort of hero, attempting to rescue the only woman he'd ever loved. The problem with that was, Ashlyn knew she wasn't. After returning home, she'd discovered he had been cheating on her pretty regularly. She'd found he'd been part of some BDSM club when she'd started clearing out his office. It had made her sick thinking about it.

Having all those unresolved emotions, which were often contradictory, wasn't easy, and that was why she began to go to therapy.

"In a way, it's easier that Paul is dead because that's definite proof he can't hurt us anymore, or anyone else," Ashlyn told her therapist during their usual session. She usually tried not to talk about Mason at these and focused mostly on recovering from the trauma Paul had put her through.

Doctor Beck was in her late fifties, a professional who dealt with this type of trauma, and her gentle voice always managed to soothe Ashlyn like nothing else could. Especially during the episodes of panic attacks.

Doctor Beck nodded. "What's the other side of that coin?"

Ashlyn shrugged. "None of us feel as though we got the justice we deserved."

All the people around them, as well as the media across the country, had learned the truth and knew Paul was a complete monster, but at times, it felt like it wasn't enough. Ashlyn had wanted him to spend the rest of his life in prison. She wanted him to feel how they felt. She was not proud of it, but she had been looking forward to seeing him behind bars, maybe with a giant cellmate who took a particular liking to him, for as long as he lived. None of that was possible now since he'd chosen the easy way out.

That made her angry.

"Tell me this. Would your everyday life change even if that were the case, if you got your desired scenario?" Doctor Beck wondered.

That resonated with her, so Ashlyn thought about it. If Paul were alive, then that would mean they would have to go through the trial. They would all have to testify and be forced to relive each portion of their imprisonment, all while looking at his smug face.

Then there was the possibility that he wouldn't get the sentence they all knew he deserved, because the judicial system was unpredictable at times. With him alive, the media would focus on his side as well. There were a lot of sick people who worshiped monsters, rapists, and murderers. Paul would get his own fan club, maybe even a documentary on crime TV, and that would be painful to endure.

"I guess in some ways, our lives would be more difficult with him still alive, but nothing major would change. I wouldn't change."

Doctor Beck nodded. "Precisely."

"Maybe it's time I accept that this was for the better," Ashlyn said eventually.

"You'll get there," her therapist encouraged. "Now, how about we deal with a little bit more today?"

Ashlyn frowned. She didn't want to talk about Mason.

Dr. Beck smiled. "I know you don't think you're ready, but you need to talk about him."

Ashlyn still felt so conflicted over Mason. She felt guilty

for thinking he was the monster behind it all, angry at him for cheating on her, grateful that he tried to rescue her, and sad that he was gone. "I've tried reconciling my feelings, but I'm still so angry at him," she shared.

"I can see that. Have you spoken to his mother again?"

A smile touched her lips. "Yes. That's one good thing that's come out of all this. His mom and I have gotten to be pretty close. I met his sister too. I wish Mason could have made up with them."

"Mason had his faults. I'm not going to deny that, or disrespect the feelings of anger you have toward him and the way he acted, but I think you need to forgive yourself and him. You both made mistakes and, in the end, his love for you was enough for him to try to rescue you."

She wasn't wrong, Ashlyn admitted, if only to herself. "I'll think about it."

Checking the clock on the wall, Dr. Beck said, "Very well. It seems our time is up anyway, but I want you to think about this some more so we can continue discussing it during our next session. I want you to focus on all the things that changed, no matter how big or small, and tell me how life became better in the last four months."

"Okay." Ashlyn wasn't particularly happy about being given homework, yet she would do everything that needed to be done to get better; to stop having nightmares; to stop being triggered by certain things, and so on.

"And you don't have to restrain yourself in your thoughts," Doctor Beck added as an afterthought.

Ashlyn nodded, collecting her things. "Okay, Doc. I'll do that."

"See you next week."

"See you, and thanks."

As she walked out of the office, she realized her life had improved a great deal in the last four months. And not because she was no longer chained in a basement. As the doctor had said, it had improved in various small ways.

For example, she'd become even closer to her family, especially Karina. They'd stopped fighting, and tackled each problem in front of them as a team. Although Ashlyn still had vivid dreams in which Paul tormented her and told her she would never be able to escape him, they didn't affect her in the same way they had four months ago. She was stronger now and looked at it differently.

Those were not the only ways her mind tormented her so she would never forget the horrors. Those were reminders that she had been strong enough to escape and defeat him.

Paul had no control over her anymore, and she was grateful for that.

And as she'd told Dr. Beck, she now had Mason's mom and sister in her life too, and they brought her a great deal of joy as well.

Checking the time, Ashlyn realized she would be late for her coffee date with Karina if she didn't hurry. Although she'd moved back to her parents' house and saw her sister every day, it was nice to get out of the house every once in a while, to talk. Especially since there were some topics they tried to avoid around the house.

As expected, Karina was already sitting in the coffee shop, enjoying the sun.

"It's done," Ashlyn announced, sitting down.

"What?"

Ashlyn rolled her eyes. "I'm signing the papers tomorrow."

"Really?"

"Yeah. Patrick called me before I went to see Doctor Beck."

Mason's fortune had finally finished probate, and all the estate and money had ended up in Ashlyn's hands. At first, she didn't want anything to do with it, thinking maybe it was what had corrupted Mason and caused him to cheat on her in the first place. However, after speaking with Karina, her parents, and of course, Doctor Beck, she came to terms with the idea that she could do a lot of good with that kind of money. Especially since she'd inherited hundreds of millions of dollars. She was now one extremely wealthy woman.

She still felt dizzy just thinking about the sum of money she was getting. She'd honestly never known Mason was quite so rich. It went without saying that Ashlyn didn't plan on keeping it all.

She had also spoken with Patrick about Mason's architectural firm, and he reassured her the rest of the associates would be more than happy to buy her out. The firm had suffered a great deal and lost business because Mason was one of the top designers in the firm, but his partners and the employees were still optimistic that they could turn things around with some rebranding, a name change, and things like that. She wished them all the best.

"So, what are your plans?" Karina asked, snapping her from her thoughts. "What are you going to do about the house?"

The house had once been her dream home. The home she'd planned to build a family in. It held no good memories for her though. Every time she entered it, all she could see was Mason's infidelity. His harsh words, his secrets. She had to let it go. She couldn't live in that house.

"Sell it, I think."

Karina nodded. "Maybe you should remodel it first?"

"Why?"

Smiling, Karina said, "To use as your showcase to get your interior design business back up and running."

Ashlyn laughed. "You're right. What do you think I should do to it?" How to destroy the bad and at the same time preserve the good? The house was beautiful; perhaps some other family could be happy there. Maybe after she remodeled it, it would be even better.

"Fill the man cave with concrete?"

Ashlyn shook her head. That damn basement room was what she felt had caused all the problems in her marriage in the first place. "Now there's an idea."

"Maybe someone at the firm could help turn it into a bonus room? Make it a part of the house's attraction or something. I mean, people really like those kind of things," Karina thought out loud.

"That's a great idea, actually," she agreed, and it matched what she was thinking about. Turn a negative into a positive.

"I know," Karina replied, grinning. "Now all that's left is to decide what to do with all that money," she teased.

"That's easy," Ashlyn said with a small shrug. "Like we talked about, I'm going to sell everything and redistribute a good portion of the wealth. Part is going to charity, and I'm giving some to Charlene, Olga, Natalie, and Amanda."

She knew that money wouldn't fix everything and couldn't change the past, but she hoped it would provide at least a small amount of peace of mind to Paul's victims. Ashlyn knew Charlene struggled with tuition, so maybe she could use this money and go to college without worrying about how many part-time jobs she would have to manage to get by.

"And the rest?"

"Buy a fancy house for Mom and Dad, and homes for you and me, along with setting up trusts for each of us." That way, they could all be close by, yet have their individual spaces and have the money to maintain easy, upper-middle-class lives.

Karina placed a hand across her heart, clearly touched. "You really have thought of everything."

"I've had plenty of time to do that," she replied somewhat sheepishly.

"How about a vacation as well?" Karina suggested.

"As long there are no men around, I'm in," Ashlyn replied without a thought.

Although she was better, she struggled with a lot of issues. At the moment, she needed space and felt skittish in the presence of men. She wasn't even sure she would be able to fully fix that, ever. At least, that was how she currently felt. Paul had scarred her for life. And no matter how she hated that was the case, it was still true.

Perhaps one day, she would be able to trust again, date again, yet that day was far in the future.

"You mean like a lesbian cruise?" Karina offered.

Ashlyn couldn't help but laugh. "We'll think of something."

"I'll drink to that."

Ashlyn nodded. That was the luxury they now had—to laugh, plan, and enjoy life. It had almost been taken away from them, but they'd fought back and won. The biggest gift she had in life at the moment wasn't the money. It was the knowledge that she was strong enough. That no matter what life decided to throw at her, she would win.

Because she already had.

THANK YOU FOR READING

Did you enjoy reading *The Dream Home*? Please consider leaving a review on Amazon. Your review will help other readers to discover the novel.

ABOUT THE AUTHOR

Theo Baxter has followed in the footsteps of his brother, best-selling suspense author Cole Baxter. He enjoys the twists and turns that readers encounter in his stories.

ALSO BY THEO BAXTER

Psychological Thrillers

The Widow's Secret

The Stepfather

Vanished

It's Your Turn Now

The Scorned Wife

Not My Mother

The Lake House

The Honey Trap

If Only You Knew

The Dream Home

The Detective Marcy Kendrick Thriller Series

Skin Deep - Book #1

Blood Line - Book #2

Dark Duty - Book #3

Kill Count - Book #4

Printed in Great Britain
by Amazon